NEWTON, KANSAS

To
Pat

NEWTON, KANSAS

The Wickedest Town in the West

JAMES I. MCARTHUR

TATE PUBLISHING
AND ENTERPRISES, LLC

Published by Tate Publishing & Enterprises, LLC
127 E. Trade Center Terrace | Mustang, Oklahoma 73064 USA
1.888.361.9473 | www.tatepublishing.com

Tate Publishing is committed to excellence in the publishing industry. The company reflects the philosophy established by the founders, based on Psalm 68:11,
"The Lord gave the word and great was the company of those who published it."

Book design copyright © 2013 by Tate Publishing, LLC. All rights reserved.
Cover design by Jan Sunday Quilaquil
Interior design by Jomar Ouano

Published in the United States of America

ISBN: 978-1-62746-187-0
1. Fiction / Westerns
2. Fiction / Action & Adventure
13.06.13

DEDICATION

This book is dedicated to my wife, Shiela Kay (Cromwell) McArthur

PROLOGUE

Two men sat on their horses looking out over the prairie, cradled on the west by a slow-moving creek around thirty feet wide. The grass was so tall it tickled the bellies of their ponies. Several large cottonwood trees stood along the riverbank, but other than that there was nothing to obstruct the magnificent view of the meadow from where they sat to the far horizon, where the golden color of the grass met the deep blue of the sky. It was the spring of 1870.

"So, Judge, you think this is the place?" asked the slimmer and younger one.

"That I do, Lakin. I've spent a week looking over this part of the territory, and I believe right where we are now would be the ideal spot for this new town of yours."

Judge R. W. P. Muse, a distinguished Union Army veteran and a probate judge currently living in Abilene, Kansas, had been hired by the Atchison, Topeka, and Santa Fe (AT&SF) Railway to recommend a site for the creation of a new town—a railroad town that would be a major hub on their line heading into the west and southwest. He was a distinguished-looking gentleman in his fifties, with sharp features projecting from a receding hairline. His beard and mustache were a mixture of black, gray, and white, while his hair was still mostly black.

"Right here is where your railroad will meet with the Chisholm Trail," the judge said. "A good place to swap out your crews going east or west, and for housing corporate offices and maintenance workers."

"And for intercepting all those cattle coming up from Texas to Abilene," Lakin said. D. L. Lakin was the commissioner of land development for the AT&SF, charged with the task of laying out the route for the new railroad. He was a head shorter than the judge, skinny as a sapling, with thinning brownish hair and a reddish complexion.

"You are in the right place for that," Judge Muse said. "Old Jessie Chisholm blazed this path himself when he was taking wagons to the Indian nation. I reckon over a million beevies have come up on this road since then, on their way to Abilene."

"Those cattle, or beevies as you call them, aren't going to Abilene for long, my friend, not for long," Lakin replied. He, as did his companion, wore a dark-blue suit and white shirt with tie. The flaps of his jacket blew gently in the morning breeze.

"In less than a year, our railroad will be passing through this very spot on its way to Santa Fe. As you know, track has already been laid to Emporia. When it gets here, it will be the new 'end of the trail' for those Texans and their cattle drives. I reckon the Kansas Pacific Railroad up at Abilene won't be too happy about that."

After a minute, he continued, "Seems to me you are right, Judge. This will make a good site for a new town, one that will be a central hub for the railroad. It's got good water all around with creeks and tributaries. What's the name of that creek over there again?"

"Sand Creek," his companion replied.

"Ah yes, Sand Creek. But you know, Judge, we're looking for more than just a railroad town. The government has given us thousands of acres of land, as an inducement for building the railway, to sell at reasonable prices to encourage development of this wide-open prairie. We need a place right in the middle of things to set up our land sales office. Seems to me this fits that bill as well. The gateway to the Arkansas Valley."

Looking back over his shoulder, Lakin said, "How do you think those people living over there will react to us building a town here?"

"Reckon it will be good news for them." There were half a dozen tents on the meadow that had only recently been erected and one wooden structure. "I think speculation on a new town has already begun, ever since word got out that the railroad would be headed this way. One of those fellows says he's been counting on just that. He moved that frame building here from Darlington township, which is east a few miles, just last month. Says he's going to set up a blacksmith shop."

"The cattle business will get this town off to a good start, Judge, but we both know that won't last. The railroads are expanding rapidly. Won't be too long before we're all the way down to Texas, I would suspect. No, the future of this little town will be in people, not cattle. People and farming."

"Couldn't agree with you more, Lakin."

"What we need is to encourage citizens to settle in these parts. Farmers and merchants. The railroad will need a commissioner for land development for this part of Kansas, and I can't think of a better candidate for the office than you, Judge. How about it? Like to work for the AT&SF?"

"Lakin, I believe this town and surrounding country have a great future, a future that is just now being born. I'd consider it an honor to be a part of that growth. By the way, do you have a name in mind for this community you're about to create?"

"I do. Most of our stockholders are from Newton, Massachusetts. It's a pleasant community, and I think it would be appropriate to name this town after them."

Lakin once again gazed out at the prairie with its tall grass and deep blue sky. "I can visualize it now. Newton, Kansas, the prettiest little town in Kansas."

The new town would be built, but not quite as the two men envisioned. It was born in blood and violence and was soon to become known as Newton, Kansas, "the wickedest town in the West."

Chapter 1

"Easy there, easy does it," Ted Baker cautioned. Ten men were pushing the frame of the front end of a store upright to nestle snuggly against the wooden floor. "Okay, that's good. Hold it right there while I nail in these braces."

The dusty street was filled with people, some engaged in constructing new buildings, and others standing around and offering unwanted advice, while dozens of men and women hurried along in every direction on some mission of their own. Horses were pulling wagons loaded with lumber, furniture, and appliances up and down the street in both directions. The clear, spring air reverberated with the sound of hammering, sawing, and excited chatter mixed with an occasional oath. Even the dogs moved as if driven by some purpose of their own. In the summer of 1871, Newton, Kansas, was a town that was a beehive of activity and growing rapidly.

Ted was a lanky young man in his early twenties, with coal-dark hair that continually fell down over his forehead. His nose was prominent, and his mouth was usually spread wide in a friendly smile. It was his eyes that disclosed his character, however. They exuded intelligence, warmth, and a keen sense of humor. Those who met him took an instant liking to his contagious energy and personality.

Now he surveyed the upright frame that would be the front of his bakery.

"Well, Pedro, what do you think?" he said to the small man standing next to him. He had hired several men to help with the construction, including this wiry, middle-aged Mexican who had only recently come up from the border seeking employment. He claimed to be a cowboy but had no horse or saddle. In spite of this, Ted found himself relying more and more on the skills and dedication of this self-proclaimed *vaquero*.

"Si, senor. I think this will be a handsome store and will serve you well. You will soon have the entire town eating your bread and biscuits. But I think maybe you should build a *horno* behind your bakery so that you could also make Indian bread and fry bread. Very good, I think."

"Horno? What in thunder is a horno?"

"A horno, senor, is an adobe oven the Indians have used for many years. It is made of clay and straw. I have never tasted a bread so good as that made in such an oven by the Pueblo Indians."

"That may be, Pedro. But for now we'll settle for a brick oven in the back of the store."

Ted looked down the street from where his shop would soon be standing. Already there was a merchandise store that was open for business, a livery stable, a blacksmith shop, holding pens for the cattle to the west, a stage station, and a new land office just opened by the Atchison, Topeka, and Santa Fe Railway. A law office was due to open for business by the end of the month.

Looking at the vigorous activity in the new town, Ted made a decision he had been thinking about for the last several days.

"Pedro, when we finish building my store, would you consider staying on and working for me in the bakery? I will need someone I can depend on to help run things. And you can build a 'horno' out in back, and we'll sell that bread along with what we bake inside."

Pedro gave this serious thought for almost one full second before he replied, "Si, Senor Ted. I would be honored to work for you. I have no one waiting for me in Mexico, and I think this will be a fine town in which to live."

"It is that," Ted replied. "Just look at that new well the railroad put in on Fifth Street. Best water I've ever tasted. That well will be the lifeline for this town. And I think our new post office is just about completed. The postmaster is someone named Johnson. Haven't seen him around as yet, though."

Just then the air was shattered by the sound of gunfire on the southern end of the dirt road, where saloons and dance halls were being built even faster than the stores and shops here.

"It is probably just a cowboy who has had a little too much tequila," Pedro said. "A new bunch of cattle arrived yesterday."

Ted gazed toward the southern part of the new town with a frown on his forehead. "I guess if we want their trade, we need to put up with their exuberance," he said. "But I don't like it. Those Texans are the wildest bunch I have ever seen. Every darn one of them carries a pistol, and soon as he's had a little liquor, he seems to think he's got to go terrorizing the town."

"What you say is true," Pedro replied. "But these hombres have been in the saddle many days and many nights, sleeping on the ground, eating beans and dust for almost two months. It is time for them to let off a little— what do you say—hot air."

"Steam," Ted replied. "Letting off steam. Guess you're right, but somebody's going to get hurt. That's the one trouble we've got to solve in our new town. We don't have any kind of law, only the federal marshal down in Wichita who comes around only when he has to."

The gunshots to the south gave way to loud voices and a woman's scream. A man came running up the street. "A cowboy's been shot," he yelled. "Any doctors up here?"

"None here," Ted said. "What happened?"

"Couple hombres got into an argument over a woman," the man replied. "It was a fair fight, but one of them has been hit badly. Doubt that he'll make it, even if there is a doctor."

"That's the third shooting in the past week," Ted said. "And most of them over some female. I swear, I doubt there are a half dozen virtuous women in the whole darn town. At least to the south of where the train tracks are going to be laid."

"Si, Senor Ted," Pedro replied. "But I think some of them are very nice."

Ted looked closely at Pedro. "I'll not even ask how you might have come by that knowledge," he said with a broad grin.

Pedro also had a wide smile on his face. "And what is it with you, senor? Do you have a woman somewhere?"

"Si, Pedro. Back in Saint Louis. She is a beauty. She and I grew up together. Soon as I get settled here, I'm going to have her come for a visit."

"And what is the senorita's name?"

"Linda. Linda Samuels."

Later in the afternoon Ted strolled down the street to the new post office. The door was open, so he walked in. It looked like everything was pretty much in order and was just about ready to open for business. There was a counter at the back of the room and behind it a tall cabinet with pigeonhole compartments for mail. A young girl was busy placing things in a drawer and arranging larger items on the counter top. She was not tall, about five feet, but her body was well proportioned. She was wearing a pair of faded jeans and a checkered shirt. Her hair was light brown, tied in a ponytail, and her nose was covered with freckles. She was not what one would call a classic beauty, but nonetheless attractive in a fresh, spirited way.

"Excuse me," Ted said. "I'm looking for Mr. Johnson. Is he in?"

"Well, if you mean my dad, no, he's not been around at all."

"That must mean you're his daughter," Ted replied, immediately realizing how stupid this sounded.

"I guess logically that would follow." She had an amused twinkle in her eyes.

Ted, feeling even more awkward, said, "Well, I'm looking for the postmaster. Is he in?"

"Sorry, no postmaster here." She was not being helpful.

"The post office in which we are standing," he said, "is just about to open. That must mean that we've got a postmaster around here somewhere."

"Nope. No postmaster, but we have a postmistress. That would be me. Jenny Johnson." She extended her hand with a big smile, and after only a moment Ted reached out and shook it.

"And you are?" she asked.

Ted was mildly embarrassed, fearing that he had sounded like a country bumpkin. "Ted Baker. I have the bakery up the street that will be opening in a few days. I hope you'll excuse my confusion. I just wasn't expecting an attractive young girl to be running a business in this wild place. You'll need to be careful around here, Miss Jenny Johnson."

"Oh, I can take care of myself. I know things are a little hectic right now, but isn't it exciting to be part of something brand new, to watch a town being born, to see it grow and mature? Or are you like a lot of the people here—just around for a fast buck and then on to the next hot spot?"

Ted laughed. "No, I'm here for the long haul. Like you, I'm enthusiastic about this town. My folks have a bakery back in Illinois and wanted me to go into business with them. But things there were too sedate, too predictable. I wanted a little more adventure, I guess."

"I reckon you came to the right place then. May be more adventure than you bargained for. But that will change with time."

"It will. They'll be laying track on to Dodge City before we know it. And I've heard some talk about a spur being built down to Wichita. If that happens, that's where the cattle drives will head. But the railroad will still be here, and acres and acres of good farm land. Eventually our little town will settle down and become respectable."

Ted was happy to find someone who felt as he did, who shared a vision of what the community would become. They continued to discuss the future of the new settlement, problems they were having in getting construction supplies, concerns over the wild cowboys coming in off the trail, and the need for law and order.

Finally Ted got around to the purpose of his visit. "I saw the mail wagon coming in a few hours ago. Just wondered if there might be any mail for me."

"Let me look." Jenny picked up a pile of letters and started to look through them. "Haven't had a chance to sort them yet." She pulled one letter from the group. "Looks like just this one," she said, and she handed it to Ted.

"Thanks." Ted glanced at the envelope and said a little self-consciously, "Looks like my fiancé hasn't forgotten me."

Jenny gave him an amused smile as he backed out of the front door.

CHAPTER 2

The night was clear with a full moon starting to rise over the low hills to the east. Buck McNurty rode along the perimeter of cattle, sitting astride a strawberry pony with a splash of white across its forehead. As he meandered among the animals, he alternately sang in a soft, low voice "Skip to the Lou My Darling" or talked to the more restless ones in a gentle voice.

There were over 2,500 Texas longhorns in the herd. At least that was the number they had started with three months ago in Austin. Buck wasn't sure just how many they might have lost along the trail, but it had been a good drive, and he figured they were probably missing no more than a dozen head.

Today had been hard, first getting the herd across the Cimarron River and then plodding along another ten miles in hot, 100-degree heat. It had cooled some after the sun went down, but the humidity was still oppressive, making Buck's shirt stick to his back from grime and sweat.

The herd belonged to seven ranchers in Texas, each animal bearing the brand of its owner. Buck and his companions were trailing the herd to Kansas for a contract drover, who had negotiated a price of $1.50 per head from the owners of the stock. There were eleven cowboys managing the herd, not counting the cook, and a wrangler looking after the forty-four horse remuda. Buck was the trail boss for the trip, having made a similar drive to Abilene the year before. Most of the waddies, as the cow herders were called, were young boys in their teens, although four were around Buck's age, twenty-two, and one was a relatively old man in his late forties.

Buck was of medium height with a slim, hard body. His face was dark from the elements, usually caked with sweat and dirt, and there were wrinkles around his eyes from squinting at the sun day after day. But beneath this weathered exterior were the lines of a handsome young man. His eyes were as blue as the sky and displayed a warm and good-natured disposition, even as the grim lines of his mouth revealed a determination to achieve whatever goal he set out to do. As the old expression went, he was a man to ride the trail with.

Buck figured they had about sixty miles to go before reaching the railroad at Newton. Four or five more days. Buck looked forward to the end of the trail but also wondered what he would do when the drive was over.

He had no family and no particular plan for his life. He had come west from his home in Illinois looking for two men. He didn't know their names or what they looked like, but if he ever found them, he would kill them on sight. Now, however, after three years, he had about given up his quest. It was time he got on with his life, but he couldn't decide just what that life should be. He only knew he didn't want to trail another herd up the Chisholm Trail. But to do what? He had no answer.

A shadow in the early darkness of the night moved up on his left. It was Tommy Richardson, a fourteen-year-old boy and one of his crew.

"Evenin', Mr. McNurty," he said. "I've come to take over the watch from you."

"Hi, Tommy. Everything's pretty quiet, but I see some flashes of light way off to the west. Someone's getting a storm, but likely it won't move in on us. If it does, you wake me pronto. I don't want to lose any doggies in a stampede at this late date."

"You got it, Mr. McNurty. I'll sure enough let you know."

Buck rode into their night camp, unsaddled his horse, and turned it into the remuda. There was a fire by the chuck wagon with three men sitting around drinking coffee.

"Hi, boss," one of them called out. "Better grab a cup and try some of this old gut warmer. It'll make your toes curl up in pure delight, I swear."

The speaker was Tim Martin, Buck's right-hand man on the drive. Tim was a tall, lanky cowboy about Buck's age who had been raised in Texas and was about as good a man with a horse and a steer as Buck had ever seen. He had a large nose, which seemed to be the highlight of his face, and a thick curl of black hair that always hung over his forehead even when wearing a hat. This had earned him the nickname of "Curly." He was a good man with a steady disposition and optimistic outlook on life. He was also handy with the guitar and often on the trail had entertained the crew with some of his songs.

The others around the camp fire were Jimmy Nelson, a fifteen-year-old kid from Texas; John Thompson, the old man on the drive, and more commonly referred to as "Gramps"; and Marty Fitzpatrick, who was several years older than Buck. Marty had signed up for the drive at the last minute and was a sour, complaining man with a cruel streak to his nature. Buck didn't much care for Marty, but he carried his share of the chores and was good with the cattle.

"Did you light that fire on purpose, or did it just naturally flare up from the heat?" Buck said.

"I think Cookie threw a couple sticks this direction and they accidentally rubbed against each other and—*wham*—the fire was there," Curly replied. "Anyway, it feels good. Dries up some of the moisture in the air."

In spite of the good-natured bantering, Buck sensed an uneasiness in the small group. Jimmy was staring at the ground and shuffling his feet as if he wished he were somewhere else, and Gramps and Marty both had a venomous look in their eyes as they glared at each other.

"Did I interrupt something?" Buck asked.

"Nothing serious," Curly said. "Gramps and Marty were just in a little disagreement as to how many of the sights Jimmy ought to take in when we get to Newton."

"Marty wants to ruin this here kid for sure," Gramps said, "and show him all the vices that will be waiting there. Jimmy just needs to pocket his wages and head straight back to his mother in Texas."

"Gramps, you're so straight laced a real man can hardly stand it," Marty said. "This here boy's been eating dirt and sleeping on the ground for the last twelve weeks, and I intend to show him a good time when we get to town."

"Marty, I'm telling you to leave this kid alone. He don't need you to show him nothing."

"I don't cotton to anyone telling me what to do or not," Marty said, "and I especially don't intend for any old man to stick his nose in my business. You're nothing but an old has-been anyway, too old to remember how to have a good time."

"Guess I'd rather be a has-been than a never-was," Gramps replied, and he took another sip from his tin cup.

Marty's face turned an ugly red, and he jumped up in front of Gramps, spread his feet, and assumed a menacing stance.

"That does it, you old coot. How about it? Got the stomach to put action to where your words are?"

Buck set his coffee down, rose to his feet, and faced Marty. His lips were curled in a slight smile, but there was no humor in his voice. "That's enough, Marty. We got our hands full just getting these cattle to market. We don't need to create any more problems than we already have. But if you feel the need to square off against somebody, how about facing me?"

Marty stood for a minute, his face crimson with barely suppressed rage. His hand moved slowly to his gun. Buck watched Marty's eyes closely. At first they were hard and bright, and Buck thought Marty might actually draw.

But then the fire went out of them, and Marty blinked. Although Marty's every instinct was to draw and have it out with his trail boss, he had seen how fast Buck was on the draw several times on their trip from Texas. There was no doubt in Marty's mind that Buck would shoot without hesitation if he made any kind of move.

After a minute, he muttered, "Our day will be coming, Buck. You and me." He turned and stomped off into the darkness.

Buck knelt back down by the fire, picked up his cup, and poured himself another coffee. He found himself almost wishing that Marty had gone for his gun. He didn't like the man and had to force himself back to his normal good nature.

"Gee wilikers, boss," Curly said. "When you get that look in your eyes, it'd scare a snake right back into his hole. I've never seen such pure determination as you just showed. You looked like a volcano about to explode. But you better watch that hombre. He's one mean critter, and he won't forget you standing him down like that."

"I don't think he'd face a man in a square fight," Buck said. "Like picking on old Gramps here. He knew Gramps's fingers are so swollen with arthritis that he can barely hold a rope. He wasn't taking much of a chance."

"Curly's right," Gramps said. "That man is just plain mean, and meanness don't happen overnight. He'd make an angry bear look mighty welcome if you had to choose between it and him."

"He always seems to be picking a fight with you, Gramps. Any particular reason that you know of?"

Gramps didn't answer for a moment and didn't look at Buck. Finally he said, "Well, we've got some history together, that man and me. I don't think he likes me knowing about that history." He didn't say anything more, and nobody around the fire inquired further. Men often came west to leave their past behind and were judged by who they were today and not by who they might have been at a different time in a different place. You didn't ask too many questions about a man's past.

After a bit, Buck said, "Curly, as soon as the sun's up, I'd like you to scout out the grass a few miles to the west ridin' parallel to the trail. Where we are now has been pretty much chopped off by drives ahead of us. We may have to move the herd over that way for the rest of the trip. Jimmy, guess it's your turn to ride drag tomorrow along with Tommy. I'll be riding point. Gramps and Marty can divide the rest of the waddies and ride flank."

"Mr. McNurty, you ever been to Newton before?" Jimmy asked.

"Well, I've been by the place. Or at least the place where I think the town is now. Wasn't anything there then but a couple of mud huts."

"Is it really going to be as wild a place as Mr. Fitzpatrick says?"

"If it's anything like Abilene, it's going to be wild. Gramps is right, Jimmy. It'll be full of gamblers and soiled doves and shysters all trying to figure ways to separate you and your wages. I promised your ma that I would look after you on the trail, and that includes trail's end. You get a bath and one home-cooked meal, and then you're on your way back to Texas."

"What about the cattle quarantine?" Curly asked. "Think we'll have any trouble on that front?"

When Texas cattle had first been brought north, some of them carried a tick to which they were immune but that infected and killed local livestock. Since then various states had imposed a quarantine on all cattle coming up from the south. And it was still a raging issue with many.

"I don't expect any trouble," Buck said. "The Kansas quarantine runs about halfway across the southern border and then straight north. Newton, like Abilene, should be just to the west of the line. Although I've heard some rumors that Illinois has passed a law that all cattle from Kansas have to be wintered here before they can be shipped into the state. Guess that's something that our boss, Hugh Anderson, will worry about." Anderson was the contract drover who had set up this drive. "Our job is over as soon as we get them settled into holding pens there at Newton."

Curly reached over and picked up his guitar, which was leaning against a log at his side, and started to plunk a few notes on the strings. "'Course we're hoping the holding pens have been built," he said. "Far as that goes, we're just hoping the railroad has been completed to this new town of Newton. Seems like we're taking a lot for granted, and I've never been one to count my chickens till all the eggs have hatched." Curly continued to strike a few strings on the guitar while he talked.

"Boss, are you going back to Texas after we get paid off?"

"No. Think I'll hang around a bit. Maybe I'll find me something to do in this brand new metropolis." Buck was still on edge from his confrontation with Marty, and he knew his rage wasn't only against Marty but had been simmering inside of him for several years. Every now and then something happened to bring it to the surface, and the intensity of it scared Buck.

"I was figuring on doing the same," Curly said. "Reckon that's where my destiny is going to be." Curly couldn't have spoken any more prophetic words.

"Hey, Curly, how about singing that song about Phyllis?" Jimmy asked. "That's one of my favorites."

"You mean 'A Song for the Southwest,'" Curly said. "You ought to know that one better'n me by now. Don't you ever get tired of it?"

"Not by a coyote's tail, I don't."

"Well, okay. Here goes."

The random plunking on the guitar gave way to a familiar tune, and Curly began to sing in a soft, low voice.

"Will you come my Phyllis dearie

To the wild mountain free.

Where the river runs so pretty,

And ride away with me…"

As the music rose over the dying flames of the fire and into the dark night, Buck felt himself beginning to unwind. Likely he'd have it out with Marty one of these days, but not here and not now.

CHAPTER 3

Ted Baker left Pedro in charge of the bakery and joined the crowd gathering at the train depot. The excitement was building as they awaited the arrival of the first train to enter Newton since the tracks had been completed. Banners were strewn across Fourth and Fifth streets, and a platform had been erected at the depot where city dignitaries sat in wooden chairs. A small band played stirring march music just to the right of the podium. July 17, 1871 was a big day in the young life of the community.

The animated chatter of the people was broken by the shrill whistle of the approaching train, and a cheer went up from the crowd.

"There she comes, boys," someone shouted as the engine and cars rounded the bend just outside of town. "The railroad's here!"

Amidst the shouts and hurrahs of the onlookers, Number 1863 of the Atchison, Topeka, and Santa Fe Railway, "Old Burnside," approached the station, slowed to a crawl, gave one last blast of steam from each side of its blackened engine, and came to a halt.

Inside the passenger car the conductor stood at the front of the cab and announced, "Here we are folks— Newton, Kansas. End of the line. Everyone disembarks. Those planning on proceeding farther west will find the stage station three blocks to the north. Have a good day."

The passenger sitting at the front of the car, facing toward the rear, made no attempt to rise from his seat or to gather his things together. He was a thin, young man with a washed-out, almost death-like color in his face, looking out at the world through watery, bloodshot eyes. The handkerchief that he clutched tightly in his left hand showed traces of blood that had appeared during one of his prolonged spells of violent coughing. He was attired in the very latest in Western wear. A broad, dark-brown cowboy hat pulled down sharply over his eyes, a tan shirt with a 'kerchief tied around his neck, and dark-brown pants with the cuffs tucked into a pair of rawhide boots. The most notable thing about his dress, other than that everything looked new and unworn, were the two Sharp 44s he had around his waist, with the thongs of the holsters tied tightly around his thin legs.

The lady sitting across from him rose and spoke to the younger women across the aisle. "Okay, ladies. Here we are. Don't forget your bonnets." All three were dressed in garish, bright, flamboyant dresses, and all three had wide-brimmed hairpieces with red and black feathers draped over the tops, which they were now donning. They were the first to depart. As the middle-aged one, who was obviously the one in charge, moved into the aisle, she gave a last sympathetic look at the young man who sat across from her. It was obvious that he was a sick man, and although they had barely spoken, she found herself feeling sorry for him.

Behind the three women, who might have been assumed to be "soiled doves" of the West, came two cowboys. Unlike the man watching them, their clothes were streaked with dirt, and well worn. Each of them had a gun belt strapped around his waist, but the holsters were not tied down, and seemed to be a more natural part of their dress than did the twin revolvers on the thin man's hips. They wore broad-rimmed hats, somewhat frayed, indicating many hours of exposure to sun, wind, and rain. The hats were pushed back somewhat jauntily on their heads. Without thinking, the hand of the young man went up to his own hat and pushed it back higher above his eyes.

Then followed a man neatly dressed in a black derby, light-blue vest, and black pants carrying two suitcases. On the side of each bag was engraved the words *Dr. Preston's Healing Tonic Water*.

He gave the young man a broad smile as he passed and headed for the exit.

Bringing up the rear were four people. Two men dressed in black with Lincoln-style black hats and sprouting black and dark red beards respectively. Accompanying them were two women, also dressed in black, and wearing black and white bonnets tied around their chins. The first was young and very pretty, the young man noticed, and the other, although much more matronly, could also be classed as noticeably attractive.

The wife and daughter of one of the men, the young man decided.

When the car was empty, the young passenger rose, grabbed a bag containing his belongings, and proceeded to the exit. He stepped off the train, looked around, and felt a thrill of excitement. There was a contagious excitement emanating from the crowd. The band was playing a tune called "Dearest Mae," a song the young man recognized to be about the girls of Baltimore. To the north along a dusty street were five or six new stores. The biggest was the Pioneer Store offering general merchandise. Next to it was a bakery, and across the street was a post office and blacksmith shop. Other buildings were going up that were in various stages of completion. Several wagons were coming down the dirt road, and there were a considerable number of people moving here and there along the street. Lumber for new buildings lined the streets.

Three railroad cars sat on a side rail to the west. The young man, whose name was Jim Riley, assumed these were being used as railroad offices and housing for railroad workers.

To the south of the tracks, there was even more activity. Saloons, dance halls, eating establishments, and hotels lined the boulevard, with names like the Red Front Saloon, Dew Drop Inn, the Gold Room, Tuttle's Dance Hall, and the Side Track Saloon. There were over fifteen buildings on this side of the tracks dedicated to providing amusement in various forms for anybody looking for a little excitement.

This was Newton—the new hub where authentic cowboys were to be found. The end of the trail for countless cattle drives coming up from Texas. Jim Riley took a deep breath and tried to stifle the ever-constant cough always in his throat. Maybe his health wouldn't permit him to live out his dream, but he could do the next best thing and mingle here with real cowhands and imagine that he was one of them.

Jim got a firm grip on his bags and headed south, into what was becoming known as the Hyde Park area—a play on the word *hide* because that's what everyone did when some of the Texas cowhands had a few drinks and started to shoot up that part of town. His first order of business was to find a room and rest up and try to bring his persistent coughing under control.

Later in the day he felt much better, got dressed, strapped his two guns onto his side, and sauntered forth into the evening. It had cooled down some, but the humidity was high, making it uncomfortable. He stood for a few minutes looking down the dirt street at the dozens of saloons and gambling establishments, taking in the sounds that filled the night air. Honky-tonk piano music, loud voices, and laughter seemed to pour from every building. Finally he decided on Tuttle's Bar, which seemed to be the busiest and loudest, and walked in through the swinging doors and headed to the bar. It was crowded, and he had to go all the way to the end of the counter to find an open space. He hesitated a minute on his order—whisky was supposed to be bad for him—but finally asked for a glass of bourbon. He was going to live it up.

He took a sip from his drink and then turned to survey the crowd. To his right was a giant faro wheel with a crowd of cowboys gathered around. Nearby was an oval poker table with five men sitting around it. Most of the players were young cowhands in well-worn jeans and ragged shirts, with one older man dressed conspicuously in a dark suit and large bow tie. To his far left there was a small stage with three ladies dressed in gaudy attire, dancing to a tune being played on a small piano next to the stage. At a table immediately to his left sat a woman and a man. Jim recognized her as the lady who had sat across from him on the train. He nodded at her, and she gave a smile in return. Turning to the man sitting beside her who was playing a game of solitaire, she said, "That's the boy I was telling you about. The one with consumption."

The man gave Jim a casual look and continued dealing the cards. Mike McCluskie, when he was standing, topped six feet. He had the look of a tavern brawler with a scar across his right cheek and a nose that leaned far to the left. He sported a black mustache, the tips of which drooped well below the line of his mouth. He was dressed like a gentleman, however, in a black suit, white shirt, and blue tie.

Two men entered the saloon and headed for the bar, squeezing in beside Jim, and edging him even further to the end of the counter. One was a burly man with red hair and a short, rusty-colored beard, broad Western hat, freshly laundered shirt, and faded jeans. He was young, and gave the impression of being used to the finer things in life. This was Hugh Anderson, the contract drover for whom Buck McNurty worked.

His companion was slightly taller but much slimmer, with a weathered face and deep wrinkles around his mouth. His eyes were dark, almost black, and the expression on his face most of the time was one you would expect on a man who had just lost his best friend. But occasionally it broke into a brief smile, displaying a sense of humor hardened by exposure to the wind and elements. Bill Bailey had come up with one of the first cattle drives of the season and now managed the stock pens and cattle awaiting shipment to Chicago.

"I tell you, Bill," Hugh was saying, "this is one of the best deals I've ever handled. I have three drives comin' in—almost five thousand cattle in all. At $1.50 per head, I'm making better than $7,500. Allowing $2000 for expenses I figure I'll clear around $5,000. Not too bad for one summer's work."

"How much you paying your drivers?" Bill asked.

"My trail boss gets $100 per month, the wrangler $50 for looking after the remuda, the waddies mostly $40 a month, and the cook $75. I figure the cook is the second most important hand on the drive."

"You were the trail boss on your first drive. Any trouble with Indians coming through the Territory?"

"Not a lot," Hugh replied. "We gave the Comanche a dozen head as a toll for passing through their land. That seemed to satisfy them."

"I remember when I came up north with a herd last year," Bailey said. Every time Bailey spoke, he waved his arms in wide gestures to emphasize a point or demonstrate some antic, edging Jim further to the end of the bar. Jim finally decided he wasn't going to budge another inch and stood, sipping his drink, his elbow almost touching Bailey's back.

"Just north of Red River, this old buck comes riding up carrying his bow and arrows at the ready," Bailey continued. "You should have seen his eyes pop when I pulled leather on him. I just reached for my firing piece and…" Bailey moved his arm to grab hold of his pistol in demonstration, hitting Jim squarely in the chest and sending him sprawling onto the floor.

Bailey paused, looked down at Jim for a moment, and then turned back to Hugh to finish his story.

Jim suppressed a cough, his face turning red with embarrassment and anger. He got to his feet and, facing Bailey, spread his legs apart, his trembling hands near the two six-shooters strapped to his thin waist. "Hey, mister," he shouted, although his voice was weak.

"Mike," Rosie said, "he's going to challenge Bailey. He's going to get himself killed. You've got to do something."

"Mister," Jim shouted in a louder voice. "I'm talking to you."

Bailey turned, saw Riley standing there ready to draw iron, and laughed. "You calling me out, boy?"

As the two men faced each other, there was a loud explosion—the blast of a gun fired into the air. Instantly all chatter and activity in the establishment came to a halt, and everyone turned to see what was happening.

Mike McCluskie sat at the table with a revolver, still smoking, clutched in his right hand. "Bailey," he said in a soft voice, "in case you hadn't noticed, you knocked this poor boy to the ground with your theatrics. I think you owe him a big apology, don't you?"

Bailey glared at McCluskie, his mouth tight and his eyes burning. This was not the first time he had faced a man with a gun and not the first time he had been in an argument with McCluskie. His first instinct was to draw and have it out, but reason prevailed. You don't go up against a man when he already has his weapon free and pointed in your direction.

Finally he said, "McCluskie, you and me are headed for a showdown one of these days. You sit in here with your crooked cards taking money from hard-working cowhands just off the trail, most of them mere boys. Someone ought to tie you up to a post and whip you raw."

Hugh Anderson stepped from behind Bailey and faced McCluskie. "That goes double for me," he said. "People think us cowboys are the troublemakers. We ain't nothing compared to the slime that hangs out in some of these bars."

"Better be careful what you say, my friend," McCluskie said.

Bailey glared at McCluskie for a minute and then turned to Riley and said, "Sonny, I maybe wasn't paying attention. If I accidentally knocked you down, I apologize. Step up here, and I'll buy you a drink just to show there's no hard feelings."

"No, thanks," Jim replied. He was confused by the events and wasn't sure if he should be grateful to McCluskie for pulling him out of a tight jam or be embarrassed that he hadn't been able to handle it himself. "Guess I'll accept your apology," he added.

"Have it your way," Bailey said. He then flashed a broad smile at Rosie and tipped his hat. "Sorry if any of this upset you, ma'am. That's a mighty striking dress you're wearing, by the way." He turned his back on McCluskie and continued with his story to Anderson.

Rosie blushed slightly, hoping McCluskie wouldn't notice.

"Pull up a chair, kid," McCluskie said. "This here's Rosie Williams. I hear the two of you rode into town together yesterday."

"Glad to meet you," Rosie said. "You know, you almost made a big mistake there. That Bill Bailey is a pretty rough character. Rumored to have killed several men in gunfights. I don't think you really wanted to tangle with him."

Jim pulled up a chair and sat down. "My name's Jim Riley. I guess I ought to thank you for what you just did, but I think I could have handled it okay."

"Sure you could, kid," McCluskie replied. "It's just that Bailey and I have had several run-ins before, and I couldn't pass up an opportunity to make him eat crow."

"You been in Newton long?" Riley asked.

"Several months. I look after things at night for the railroad. Make sure nobody steals anything. And, I will admit, I like to gamble. Most of these cowboys and railroad hands think they're pretty savvy when it comes to cards, and I just have to teach them a lesson the hard way."

Riley stayed at the table with Rosie and McCluskie for more than an hour. He was fascinated by the stories Mike McCluskie told, and he felt privileged to be able to look on him as a friend.

———————

Later that evening Riley returned to the saloon and found McCluskie in the middle of a poker game with three cowboys and a Mexican laborer from the railroad. Mike was winning consistently, and the others were growing increasingly disgruntled. Abruptly McCluskie gathered in his winnings and said, "That's all for me, boys. Time to get to my night job."

"Hey, you can't leave now," one of the players said. "You got to give us a chance to get our money back."

"I don't know how to say this politely," McCluskie said with a broad smile, which accentuated the ugly scar across his right cheek, "but the way you gents play, you'd have a mighty hard time winning anything back. You're lucky I'm checking out while you still have a few dollars left."

"Seems mighty unnatural the way those cards kept falling just right for you," the cowboy to his right, who was only eighteen years old, said. "Mighty unnatural."

Mike paused in gathering his winnings, his smile replaced by a sudden cold, hard look. "Are you trying to say something, my friend, or just blubbering at the mouth?"

The cowhand's face turned red with anger. "I'm saying that it seems mighty peculiar that you kept getting winning hands while the rest of us always came up losers."

"I'll give you one chance to apologize for those words, cowboy, or else you'd better be ready to back them up the hard way."

"I ain't apologizing to you, that's for sure." The cowboy stood and reached for his gun, but he was too slow. McCluskie shot him from where he sat.

The cowhand dropped his gun, clutched his shoulder, and fell across the table.

McCluskie faced the other three players. "Anybody else got anything to say?" he asked in a brittle voice. "Speak up now, or else I better not hear any more insinuations about my honesty."

The other players didn't move or speak. One of the spectators said, "It was a fair fight. He was going for his gun." There was a general murmur of agreement from the onlookers.

After a moment, McCluskie spoke again to the other two cowboys. "If you got nothing to say, better get your friend out of here and to a doctor. He's getting blood all over the cards."

Mike placed his gun back in his holster and stormed from the saloon.

Jim Riley watched him go, a look of complete admiration showing on his pale face.

CHAPTER 4

B uck McNurty, Hugh Anderson, and Bill Bailey sat on their horses watching the last of the cattle being driven through the chute into the holding pen. It was a hot, blistering day in early August. The stench from stock pens was overwhelming and seemed to cling to the dust stirred up by the longhorns.

"Guess that about wraps it up," Hugh said. The cows were sold to a buyer from Chicago for $35/head, almost four times what they would have been worth in Texas. Hugh had paid the cowhands their wages earlier in the day, and most of them were now in town watering down their parched throats with rot-gut whiskey. Hugh gave Buck a $100 bonus for getting the herd safely to market in a timely manner.

"I'll take my contract fee out of the proceeds and send the rest of the money to the owners," Hugh said "I think they'll be happy with the results. Bill, I appreciate you getting room in the pens for these critters. We've been holding them west of town for three days now, and they were getting mighty restless."

"Just doing my job, Hugh," Bill replied. "Your timing was pretty good. Three herds came in earlier in the week, and we're just now getting them on cars headed to Chicago. Worst thing is that five drives have come in since you got here. Almost ten thousand beevies. They're having to hold them off to the west. Anymore and I'm going to send them up to Ellsworth or Abilene."

"That will add almost a week to their traveling time," Buck said.

"Well, they'll be sitting here longer than that waiting for holding pens. And the grass is getting pretty scarce around here."

"I don't envy them that trip," Hugh said. "I hear tell farmers are moving in up that way and are starting to put up wire fences to keep the cattle out. Glad we don't have many sod busters around here as yet."

"We were a little worried about the quarantine keeping our cattle out," Buck said. "Guess it didn't extend this far west."

"Not as far as Kansas is concerned," Bill said. "However, in Illinois they passed a law that all cattle have to be wintered for one year here in Kansas before they can be shipped into their state."

"How are you getting around that one, Mr. Bailey?" Buck asked.

"Why that's no problem." He gave an exaggerated wink. "We just need to have papers for each shipment stating that they've been wintered here. They're not too hard to come by." He chuckled. "And in fact many cattle really will be held here over the winter."

"Hugh Anderson here is a pretty savvy hombre," Bailey said to Buck. "He's bringing in three different drives this summer. 'Course he comes by it naturally. His dad is a big rancher down in Texas, and he's been around cattle since he was knee high to a grasshopper. Don't quite know why he left all that luxury to eat dust on the trail, but I guess that's his business."

Hugh laughed. "Man's got to make it on his own if he's got any self-respect."

"By the way, Buck," Bailey said, "if you're interested in a job, I'm always looking for a good hand to help manage the cattle once they've been turned over to me. Hugh here tells me you're a good one."

"No thanks, Mr. Bailey. I've had it up to my ears with chasing these critters around for the past few months. Think I'll just head into town and relax for a little while."

"What are your plans after that, Buck?" Hugh asked.

"Guess I don't rightly know. I ain't getting any younger. Time I settled down and started to make something out of myself. Don't think I'll head back to Texas. Time was I had a reason to be there, but that's kinda faded away by now."

Hugh nodded. He had heard that Buck was looking for two men, but he didn't know the particulars.

"If you change your mind, just let me know. Like Bill here, I can always use a good hand."

"I'll surly do that, Mr. Anderson."

"If you're headed into town, I've got just one word of advice," Bill Bailey said. "Stay away from a feller named Mike McCluskie. Especially if you've got a hankering for cards. He's got a right smart girlfriend, I'll admit, but that man's pure poison. I wouldn't trust him any further than I could throw that old bull over there. He usually hangs out at Tuttle's Dance Hall."

"I'm not much on card playing, but I'll make sure I give him a wide berth if I run into him."

———————————

Later in the day Buck rode into town. He had three goals in mind. One was to get a home-cooked meal that he could eat sitting at a table, another to find a nice soft bed under a roof, and the third was to get a warm bath and shave. As he put his horse up at the stables, he still hadn't decided on the priority of these three needs but decided the first step was to rent a room at one of the hotels. The Kansas Inn just north of the tracks seemed a likely place, and they had a vacancy sign hanging on the front porch.

After the clerk had shown him to his room, he stretched out on the bed just to see how it felt. The next thing he knew it was dark. He had slept for six hours. He thought about getting something to eat but decided he was just too dog-gone tired. He undressed, lay back down on the bed, and was asleep again in minutes.

The next morning Buck achieved the second of his goals: a nice, warm bath, followed by a shave and haircut. But he still hadn't relaxed over a home-cooked meal. Looking at himself in the mirror, Buck realized just how worn his jeans and shirt were. Those in his bedroll weren't much better. He decided that after a big breakfast he would splurge and buy some new clothes.

The dining room at the hotel was busy. Three men sat at the table nearest the entrance; a thin, pale young man was seated behind them; two women engaged in animated conversation over to the right; and two men and two women toward the rear. Buck headed to a table next to them. He needed to study the menu for only a minute before ordering a steak, three eggs sunny side up, fried potatoes, and toast.

As he sipped a cup of very black and very hot coffee, he looked around and noticed for the first time that the two men sitting at the table next to him were dressed in black suits, and both had beards—one coal black and the other reddish. The women were dressed modestly in gingham dresses with small bonnets adorning their heads. The men were discussing something in a foreign language, maybe Russian or German. One of the women seemed to be in her forties, and the other was much younger. *Mother and daughter*, Buck thought.

Just then the younger one turned slightly to make a point to the other woman, and in so doing looked directly into Buck's eyes. Buck felt like he had been hit by a bolt of lightning. He had never seen a prettier woman. She had dark hair that accentuated her pale skin and full lips. But it was the blue eyes that held him. If eyes are the windows of the soul, Buck at that moment saw everything he needed to know about this girl. Something clicked inside of him, and he knew he had to get to know this young lady.

The girl noticed Buck staring openly at her and turned away, her face reddening. A few minutes later the two men and the older woman got up to leave. The girl was still drinking coffee and stayed behind. The mother indicated she would be right back.

As soon as they left, Buck spoke to the girl. "I couldn't help but notice that you folks speak a foreign language. Are you new to the country?"

She looked at him, started to say something, and then turned away. Not to be discouraged, Buck continued. "My name's Buck McNurty. Just got into town myself. Came up on a trail drive from Texas. Had over 2,500 of those doggies to ride herd on."

The girl gave him a brief look then turned back and stared fixedly toward the front of the dining room.

After a minute, Buck said, "I thought it was going to be pretty hot today, but things seemed to have suddenly cooled down. Mighty cool." And he chuckled to himself. The girl still didn't look at him but broke into a soft laugh herself.

Finally she turned and spoke directly to him. "You must not think me rude, Mister Cowboy—whatever your name is—but where I come from, young women do not speak to strangers. We have not had the—what do you say—the proper introduction."

"Well, golly, we ought to be able to manage that."

Just then a soft voice from behind Buck said, "Ma'am, is this cowhand bothering you?"

Buck turned to find the thin young man who had been sitting at the front of the dining room standing in a tense position, feet spread, and hands hovering over two six-shooters. Buck's first instinct was to laugh, but then he noticed, in addition to the sickly complexion of the youth and the slight moisture over his lips, the intensity of his look. The young man was obviously not well but was willing to risk a showdown to defend this woman's right to privacy.

"Oh no, no," the girl was quick to say, recognizing the potential danger. "Everything is fine. There is no trouble here. We were just having the conversation."

The young man looked confused. "I saw him trying to talk with you, and you looked like you didn't want any part of him. But he kept on pestering you I thought."

"No—is no bother," she said. "We did not have the introduction for me to be talking with him. But is okay."

As she spoke, the mother came back into the dining room, scowled at both Buck and the young man, and gave the girl a questioning look.

"Here is my mama," the girl said. "We go shopping now." She rose, took her mother's arm, and the two of them left the room.

Buck looked again at the young man standing by the table, who now appeared slightly embarrassed. "My name's Buck McNurty. I'd be obliged if you would join me for a cup of coffee. Not often you meet someone willing to defend a woman's honor."

"Guess I made a fool of myself," the young man said. He pulled up a chair, extended his hand, and said, "Name's Jim Riley."

"Glad to meet you, Jim. Been in Newton long?"

"Maybe a week or so. I wanted to get a job cowboying, but my health hasn't been too great. Guess the nearest I'll ever be to a wrangler is just rubbing elbows with one. You come up from Texas?"

"Yup. Brought a herd of cattle up. Got here just a few days ago."

"I always thought being a cowboy would be a great thing. Seemed like they were real down-to-earth people. But I had a run-in a few days back with some of them, and they weren't exactly knights on horseback. Kinda changed my opinion of them. Made a new friend, though. Mike McCluskie."

Buck looked up in surprise at the name. "McCluskie. I've heard of him. Haven't heard anything very good though. You sure you want him for a friend? Way I heard it, he's a no-good card shark and a killer."

Riley bristled at the words. "I've heard some of those rumors, but he's honest, and he stood up for me when I was in trouble with those cowboys. He shot a troublemaker a few days ago, but it was a fair fight. Law won't bother him none. He's a good man, and I don't want to hear anything different."

Buck studied the young man for a moment, thought about arguing the point with him, and then decided it would do no good. "Well, if he stood by you when the chips were down, I guess he can't be all bad. Who were the cowboys you were butting heads with?"

"Two of them. One was someone named Anderson, and the other was Bill Bailey. He seems to think he's some kind of big shot around here, but I've got it on strict authority that he's killed at least five men in shootouts. Talk about Mike being a killer. Bailey's the bad one, I'm thinking."

Again Buck had to stifle his surprise. God knows there was probably some truth in what the young man said, but Bill Bailey had seemed like a decent sort. Buck decided to change the subject.

"So now you're down on all of us cowhands, I take it."

"Well, most of them anyway. Not you though. You seem like a square shooter."

"I guess us cow chasers are just about like everyone else. Some are good, some are bad, and most are somewhere in between. I'll tell you one thing though. Most of the hands I've known are hard working and uncomplaining and ride for the brand."

"Ride for the brand. What's that mean?"

"You know every rancher has a brand for his cattle. So if you ride for the brand, it means you are riding for the ranch and the owner. And not just riding, it means that you stick with the boss when times get tough. If you take a man's wages, you owe him your loyalty."

Jim thought this over for a moment. "I reckon the same thing holds true for friends. If you call a man your friend, then you ought to owe him your loyalty. That's the way it is with me and Mr. McCluskie."

Once again Buck was about to respond but thought better of it. Instead he looked at the six-shooters hanging from Riley's thin waist and said, "Tell me. You ever fired those guns?"

Riley looked a little sheepish as he replied, "You bet I have. Once anyway. Shot at some bottles back in Kansas City. But I know how to use them. I'm pretty fast on the draw."

"I'm sure you are, kid. But just remember, fast may be good, but accurate is better."

"It must be exciting to be on a cattle drive," Riley said.

"Now and then it is, when you're trying to get the critters across the river or when you have a stampede. But most of the time it's just long hours of trailing cattle, eating dust, and not getting much sleep."

"They must have a lot of cattle in Texas to have so many being brought up here. I heard last year over six hundred thousand were driven to Abilene."

"During the conflict between the states, most of the young men in Texas were off to war, and the cattle ran wild in the back brush. And multiplied. I reckon there must be several million doggies running loose, just there for anyone that wants to claim them. That's why they're not worth much down there. But in Kansas City and Chicago, those critters sell at a pretty handsome price. So ranchers started rounding them up, branding them, and trailing them here to the railroad."

"Is it hard to keep them bunched up on the trail?"

Buck laughed. "Only time we get them bunched up is at night. On the trail, we get one of the leaders to start ambling north in the morning, and the rest follow. We ride along to keep them in line and headed in the right direction. Why sometimes our herd will stretch out over a mile long. We don't rush them none. They need to be nice and fat when they get to the railroads so's they will bring a good price. We probably average only about twelve miles a day."

"If you don't mind me asking, Mr. McNurty, did you ever shoot anyone?"

"No, I never have. As a general rule, I figure fire arms are the least desirable way of settling an argument." Buck's voice took on a bitter tone. "But sometimes killing is the only way you're ever going to get justice done."

As they talked, Curly, Gramps, and the two teen-aged waddies came into the room. Buck waved them over to the table.

"Jim, I'd like you to meet some real cowboys. Each of these gents will do to ride the trail with. This here's my good friend Curly Martin. The old man is Gramps Thompson, and the two cowpokes with him are Johnnie Richardson and Jimmy Nelson. Pards, this young man is Jim Riley."

They all shook hands with Riley and pulled chairs up to the table.

"Gramps, you looking out for these two young hombres?" Buck said, indicating Johnnie and Jimmy.

"We've seen some of the sights of the town," Gramps admitted. "Even got their first taste of rot-gut whiskey last night. I figured they earned that much. But only one shot each."

"Whiskey? That's pretty strong. What ever happened to a glass of beer?"

"Boss," Curly said, "you ever tasted warm beer? Now back east I hear tell you can get it cold, but not out here in the west. I prefer a good old shot of Kentucky bourbon any day."

Buck turned to the two boys. "I hope that one shot is all you ever have a hankering for. Whiskey has ruined more good men than you'd ever imagine. Take my advice and give it a wide berth."

"Mr. McNurty," Johnnie said. "Know what we saw in the saloon yesterday? A woman smoking a cigarette. I ain't never seen a woman smoke before."

"I hope that's all you saw of that lady," Buck replied.

"Yes, sir. Old Gramps here he didn't let us out of his sight."

"Guess we'll be heading back to Texas at the end of the week," Jimmy said. "There's about a dozen of us trailers going together."

Jim Riley listened with some envy, thinking about their adventures, but didn't say a word.

"Well, it's been a real pleasure to ride with both of you," Buck said. "You tell your parents that I said you made them proud."

Just then the quiet of the dining room was shattered by two gunshots in the street. The crowd in the restaurant jumped to their feet and ran to the door to see what was happening, including Buck and everyone at his table.

In the middle of the dusty road, Marty Fitzpatrick stood, holding a bottle of whiskey in one hand and his six-shooter in the other. Facing him were the two men in black suits with dark beards who had been in the dining room earlier. To one side were the mother and the daughter. The younger one was holding her hands to her mouth with a terrified look in her eyes.

Fitzpatrick fired another round into the dirt just in front of the two foreigners. "I said I wanted to see you dance, dammit. I ain't never seen no Men-no-nite before." He drew out the word in three distinct syllables and then broke out in a loud laugh as he took another swig from the whiskey bottle. "Guess I'll have to nick your toes some to get some action here. I sure do have a hankering to see a Men-no-nite dance."

The two men did not move but stared fixedly at Fitzpatrick without expression as Marty pointed his gun at the men's feet.

Buck drew his revolver, stepped into the street, and fired a bullet an inch from Fitzpatrick's boots. Instinctively Marty jumped back.

"Looks like you dance pretty well yourself, Marty," he said. "But who wants to see a drunken sot try to do the light fantastic? I suggest you put that firing piece back in its holster and let these good people go about their business."

Fitzpatrick gave Buck a look of pure hate. This was the second time Buck had faced him, and he wanted nothing more than to raise his gun and fire away. After a long minute, he put his pistol back in its case. He had seen Buck shoot on the trail, and he doubted he was a match for him face-to-face, especially after he had been drinking.

"You been riding me for three months, McNurty, and I've just about had my fill of it. One of these days I reckon I'll have to do something about it. But this ain't the time or place."

He turned and walked a little unsteadily back into the Tuttle Dance Hall.

The two men in black looked at Buck and then turned away talking to each other, making no attempt to thank him or acknowledge what he had done. Buck hadn't expected or wanted any thanks but was surprised by their seeming indifference.

Then the young girl walked up to him. "I think the introduction we must make. My name is Katrina Dorsky, and I thank you for what you have just done, Mr.…."

"McNurty," Buck stammered. "Buck McNurty. And if we've been properly introduced, can I call you Katrina?"

Katrina gave him a wide smile and nodded her head slightly.

"We are farming people from Russia, looking for the land to buy. My parents have taken the—what do you call it—the vow against violence. That is why my father and our friend, Mr. Knopner, did not try to resist this cowboy who likes to shoot his gun and scare people. And why they find it hard to say the 'thank you' when you also used the violence in protecting them. But my mother and I thank you."

The two men were talking rapidly in German when one said something to the other, and they both started laughing.

"What are they so tickled about?" Buck said.

"They think that God maybe sent you. Mr. Knoper says that all the time they were being shot at he was saying the prayer from 140 of the book of Psalms."

"What prayer is that?"

"The prayer, it says something like: 'Keep me, O LORD, from the hands of the wicked; Protect me from men of violence who plan to trip my feet.'"

Buck laughed. "I don't know that God had anything to do with it, but I'm sure glad I happened along when I did. It got us that proper introduction."

Katrina gave him a big smile and turned back to her parents and their friend.

"That was pretty interesting, Mr. McNurty," Jim Riley, who was standing just behind Buck, said. "Maybe what you were saying about some cowboys being okay is true, but I'm still a friend to Mr. McCluskie. And as you cowboys say, I ride for the brand." He turned and walked away up the dusty street, coughing lightly and holding a blood-soaked handkerchief to his mouth.

CHAPTER 5

T ed stood in the street in front of his shop admiring the new sign. The top line read "Ted's Bakery," and underneath "Bread, Donuts, and Pastries." Today was his grand opening, and it was a huge success. He had run out of everything by ten that morning. He turned to his assistant who was standing beside him.

"Pedro, I think we need to get up even earlier tomorrow and start the ovens," Ted said. "Maybe four."

"*Si*, Mr. Ted. I think that is very early, but maybe the air she will be a little cooler."

"You're right on that one," Ted replied. At midmorning, the atmosphere was heavy with moisture, and both men were sweating profusely. Ted looked up at the sky. "Those clouds seem to be moving pretty fast. Ought to bring in some rain if we're lucky."

"You have much money from this morning," Pedro said, "but you do not carry the gun. Are you not afraid that some of these caballeros from the saloons might take it in their minds to rob you?"

"I've got that safe that came in yesterday to keep it in. It would be pretty heavy to try to haul off. And anyway, you're still wearing a pistol around your waist. I think any of those hombres you're talking about would think twice before deciding to tackle you. Come to think on it, I don't think I've ever seen you without it."

"This is a dangerous town, senor. Almost every day someone is shooting their *pistolas*. It is not wise to go unarmed."

Ted laughed. "Well, I'll leave the shooting to others. But I think maybe when we are making bread you could at least hang them on a nail someplace."

"Si, senor."

Early that afternoon Ted wandered down to the post office to see if he had any mail. Two trains were coming in each day now. The first was a mail and express with limited passenger service; the second was primarily an accommodation train. As he strolled down the dusty street, he studied the dark clouds now building to the southwest. *I better hurry, or I'll get caught in a downpour,* he thought.

When he entered the post office, Jenny was busy sorting a large stack of mail.

"Hi, Jenny. Got anything for me?"

"Well, now let me see." She pulled several envelopes from one of the pigeonholes. "Looks like an advertisement from some store back east. Copy of the *Emporia News*. And then this one." She held up a small purple envelope. "Looks like it is in a woman's handwriting." She held the letter to her nose. "Wow! Smells perfumery. I guess you are not interested in that. I'll just toss it aside," she teased.

"No you don't." Ted laughed as he grabbed the envelope from her hands. "The future Mrs. Baker would frown on that."

A loud clap of thunder shook the building, making them both jump.

"Looks like you might get a little wet going back to your shop," Jenny said. "Are you going to the meeting tonight?"

"Wouldn't miss it."

Sedgwick County, which included both Newton and Wichita, wanted to issue bonds to finance the building of a railroad spur between the two towns. A meeting was being held in Newton to discuss the proposal.

"I've got mixed emotions about it," Ted continued. "If they build the railway to Wichita, that means all the cattle trade will go there next year, which will really hurt business here. But on the other hand, I think we might be better off in the long run to rid ourselves of all these hell-raising cowpokes who come off the trail with nothing more on their minds than whiskey, women and gambling."

Jenny laughed. "What kind of spoil sport are you, Mr. Baker? After all, they've been in the saddle for three months or more. Need something to get their minds off cattle and horses."

Outside a light rain, which had started a few minutes before, suddenly turned into a torrential downpour. Ted walked over to the door and looked out.

"Would you look at that. I don't think I've ever seen it come down like this before."

Jenny joined his side and gasped. Boxes and boards were blowing down the street. Suddenly a cat tumbled down the boardwalk head over heels. Through the blinding rain they could see a large funnel coming out of the sky, headed straight for them. The wind picked up even more and rattled the windows of the building.

"We've got to find cover," Ted said. He grabbed Jenny and pulled her back from the door. Looking around, he could see no safe place to hide from the storm except to get under the counter, which was made of heavy pieces of oak. He guided her across the room, but halfway there, Jenny stumbled and fell, pulling Ted down with her. Just then the front door flew open and with a loud wrenching sound was ripped from its hinges and disappeared into the torrential rain. The wind roared through the building, picking up everything not anchored down. Letters in the mail slots were hurled through the air. One hit Ted in the cheek, its sharp corner drawing blood.

Ted began crawling to the counter, pulling Jenny with him. As they ducked under it, parts of the roof tore away. Then with a loud roar, the entire overhead was gone, and rain pounded down on them. Ted covered Jenny with his body. Debris was flying everywhere, and the sound was devastating. The wind blew even harder, and the counter tipped over and was blown to the wall. They were left unprotected. A large piece of wood slammed into Ted's shoulder, and then he felt both of their bodies being lifted off the floor by a strong suction. He looked around for something to hold on to, but there was nothing.

Then, as quickly as it came, the storm passed, and the wind died away, followed by an eerie silence.

Ted pushed a board off his back and rose unsteadily to his feet. "Are you all right?" he asked Jenny.

"I-I think so." He helped her up, and they looked around at what was left of the post office. Half of the back wall was still standing. Other than that everything had been leveled.

"All of my mail. It's all gone. Blown to who knows where," Jenny said.

She sounded so forlorn that Ted put his arm around her and held her tight. Both of them were soaked from the rain. Jenny's hair was plastered to her head, and her forehead and lips were shiny with moisture. For a moment, he thought how attractive she was, even when disheveled and dripping wet.

"Well, you may have lost everyone else's mail, but at least I got my letter from Linda before..." He looked down at his hand, which was empty. "I was holding it right here in my hand," he said.

They stood for a moment; then Jenny started giggling, and in another minute they were both laughing hysterically, releasing the tension that had built up with the storm.

———————————

Out by the cattle pens, a small crowd hovered around a figure lying prone on the ground. It was Johnnie

Richardson, the sixteen-year-old hand that had ridden with Buck on the trail from Texas. Buck was kneeling beside the boy, holding his head. Jimmy was on the other side of his friend.

"I ain't never seen anything like it, Mr. McNurty," Jimmy was saying. "That old funnel came down out of the sky lookin' just like pictures I've seen of an elephant's trunk, wiggling this way and then that way. We were hiding in a ditch, and I was holding my head. Then I heard Johnny shout he was goin' for a ride, and next thing I knew he was being lifted right up from the ground where we was layin'. I'll never forget that look on his face. He was right scared. Then he was gone. We found him a quarter mile down from here after the storm passed, his head split open. Guess he hit something pretty hard."

Johnnie moaned softly and opened his eyes. He looked at the sky and then focused with some difficulty on Buck.

"Guess I'm done for, Mr. McNurty," he whispered. "Tell my ma that I...that I...tried to live like Pa taught me." He tried to say something more, and then his body went slack. After a minute, Buck laid the boy's head back on the ground.

———————————

The tornado had touched down just outside of town, swept across the holding pens, and then cut a swath through a quarter of the business district, destroying five buildings. Fortunately Ted's Bakery had been spared, as well as the Kansas Hotel and the Pioneer General Store.

Surprisingly only nine cattle were killed, and Johnnie was the only human casualty.

By late afternoon, the sounds of hammering, sawing, and cussing could be heard floating across the damp Kansas air—the sounds of a town rebuilding after suffering a major blow. The small community was young enough and vigorous enough to take anything in stride. And at the far end of Hyde Park, someone who had enjoyed an ample amount of Irish whiskey fired a gun in the air.

CHAPTER 6

J ohnny Richardson was buried on Newton's Boot Hill the next day. Reverend George Overstreet, a visiting Presbyterian minister, led the service at the graveside. He was tall, thin, and clean shaven with a prominent nose, looking almost like a scarecrow, but he had a deep, resonant voice that rang with clarity and authority.

"Lord, we don't know why things work out the way they do. Johnnie here was a young man, a good man, although still just a boy in years. He had a whole life before him. Some might say, 'Why would you let this happen to him, Lord?' But we know we are not puppets being pulled by strings from above. You blessed us with free will, and I guess we just have to accept that we make our own decisions on when and where and how we go about our business, and sometimes that gets us in the wrong place at the wrong time. We don't have anyone jerking us this way and that from above, and I guess we wouldn't have it any other way."

Buck stood at the edge of the small crowd, hat in his hand. Gramps Thompson and Curly Martin were there, along with Jimmy Nelson.

At the end of the service, Gramps turned to Buck and said, "I been meaning to tell you. Old Bill Bailey been askin' for you. Says he's got a job for you if you're interested. Shepherding a farm family around the countryside looking for land. Seems they want someone experienced in making camp and tending to horses and savvy about being out in the wild to look after them for a few days."

Buck laughed. "No thanks. Last thing I need is to be a nursemaid to a bunch of tenderfeet."

"That's what I thought you'd say. They're foreigners anyway. Two men and two women. One of them is right good-looking though."

Buck looked up with sudden interest. "Foreigners? Men dressed in black and sporting long beards?"

"That sounds like the ones. You acquainted with them?"

"I might be. You know, maybe I should reconsider that job offer. We ought to be more welcoming to visitors from other countries."

Curly laughed. "You don't fool me, boss. You perked up as soon as you heard there was a pretty young woman involved. Can't say that I blame you, though."

Buck turned to Jimmy, placed his hands on his shoulder, and said, "Jimmy, I'm not headed back to Texas. I guess you're going to have to take the news to Johnnie's ma. Tell her he was a fine boy and that we thought highly of him." He pulled a wad of money from his pocket and counted out $100.00. "This was my bonus for the drive," he said. "I want you to take half of it and give the other half to Johnnie's parents, along with his wages and other things. Think you can handle that?"

"Yes, sir," Jimmy replied. "I'd be right proud to do that."

———————

Buck entered Ted's Bakery early the next morning. "If my eyes didn't tell me where I was, my nose sure would," he said. "Smells good in here."

"Well, if you're hankering for some pastries, you came to the right place," Ted Baker replied. "Just brought them out of the oven."

"I'm meeting some folks to discuss a business deal. Thought something sweet might help things along. I'll take a dozen of those donuts that are making my mouth water."

"One dozen donuts, coming up. Guaranteed to make any business meeting more enjoyable."

Buck watched Ted sack up the pastries. "You wouldn't by any chance hail from Illinois, would you?" he asked.

"Matter of fact I do. Sweetwater."

"Sweetwater. Well, I'll be damned. That's my old town. I thought I recognized that Illinois accent."

Ted looked hard at Buck. "As I live and breathe. I know you. Buck McNurty. You used to live on that farm just south of town."

"That's me all right. And you must be that skinny kid that worked in his dad's bakery. Ted Baker as I recall."

"One and the same. Well, it sure is good to run into some home folks out here. You look like a western man by your boots and guns. What have you been doing all of these years?"

"Oh, a little bit of everything. Just brought a herd up from Texas. Don't quite know what to do with myself now."

"I remember about your parents being killed. Never did catch the guys that did it, as I recall."

Buck paused a moment before answering. It was obvious that this was still a painful memory for him. "No. There were two of them. Apparently stopped by the farm, thought Dad might have some money around the place, so they killed both of them. For a while there I thought I might be able to track them down. That's why I came west."

"You never got a look at them, did you?"

"I was in town when it happened. Never laid eyes on either of them as far as I know. I always figured they took out for the West. They stole my dad's pocket watch. Had his name engraved on it. I had this crazy idea that someday I might just meet up with someone who had that time piece if I was in the right place at the right time."

"And did you?"

"Matter of fact, I did. An old geezer in a saloon down in Austin had it. I was about to fill him full of holes, but he convinced me that he had won it in a poker game from someone who had won it in another game. The trail just petered out. I been playing cowboy ever since."

"Sorry to hear that, Buck."

"Say, aren't you the kid that was hanging out with that good-looking town girl—Linda something, wasn't it? She was the best-looking girl I ever did see. Wonder what ever happened to her."

Ted laughed. "Linda Samuels. Matter of fact, she's my fiancée. Going to be coming out here for a visit one of these days. We haven't set the date yet for the wedding. She wasn't too keen about me coming out to the 'wilderness,' as she calls it. I'm hoping she'll get out here and see how exciting it is to be part of something brand new—building a town from scratch and watching it grow."

"Let me know when she comes. I'll be around. Sure would be nice to lay eyes on her again. You're a lucky man."

"I am that."

"Well, I'd best be getting to my meeting over in the lobby at the Kansas Hotel. How much for the donuts?"

"On the house for home folk. It's good seeing you again, Buck. Drop in whenever you get hungry."

"Hey, I think you sacked up thirteen donuts here."

"That's right. Don't you remember from Sweetwater about Baker's dozen? Always an extra for luck," Ted Baker said.

When Buck got to the hotel, he found his guests waiting in the lobby—Mr. and Mrs. Dorsky; their friend, Boris Knopner; and as he hoped, Katrina.

After the introductions, Buck opened the sack of donuts and passed them around. Katrina took a bite, opened her eyes wide, and said, "The donuts, they are very good, no?"

Buck was pleased. "Got them from Ted's Bakery down the street. Turns out he and I are from the same place in Illinois."

"This is a man I would like to meet," Katrina said. "Of course, only with the proper introduction," she added with a twinkle in her eye. "Such a man would be nice to know."

Buck was beginning to wonder if bringing the donuts had been such a good idea after all.

"You are the young man that saved us from the embarrassment of the other day," Martin Dorsky said. "You must forgive me for not properly thanking you. All of this gunplay seems so unnecessary and so foolish. But I do not think he would have actually shot my feet, as he threatened."

"I'd have to differ with you on that," Buck said. "That man is downright mean. He wouldn't have hesitated to blow your toes off."

"Well, the matter is over. We are farmers, Mr. McNurty, from Russia. We have come to this country and to this place to seek suitable farmland. We Mennonites are a peaceful people and do not believe in fighting. In Russia, we had the promise from Catherine the Great, our country's leader, that we would never have to serve in the army, but things are changing. Now Alexander is our ruler, and he tells us that we must be soldiers for Russia. This we cannot do. Your country offers assurances that we will not have to serve in the military, so we have come to inspect the land. We have been to many parts of your country, but we find the land and climate here most like our homeland in Russia."

"I guess the price of land around here must be pretty reasonable," Buck said.

"Your president wants to see this land developed. First must come the railroad to allow access to the land. Then must come people to settle in the land. Your government has given large land grants to the railroad to encourage them to build the tracks to this undeveloped territory. The railroad in turn offers the property for sale at very low prices to encourage the people to come. We can buy good farmland at $2.50 per acre. We believe this is a most attractive offer. But we would like to inspect the land for ourselves."

Buck stole a look at Katrina. She looked very serious, a slight frown in her forehead. Buck couldn't decide if she was prettier the way she looked now or when she smiled.

"You keep saying 'we,' Mr. Dorsky," Buck said. "Are you speaking for more than just you and Mr. Knopner?"

"Yes. If we find suitable land, many from our village will come. We are encouraged by what we see here but would like to inspect the land to the west—say thirty or forty miles—then make a wide sweep to the north and to the east. But we are strangers in a new land, Mr. McNurty, and would like to have an experienced person accompany us to help with the directions and with making the camp at night. My wife and daughter will go also, and they will do all of the cooking. Judge Muse, who runs the AT&SF Land Office, and a Mr. Bailey have recommended you. Would you be interested?"

Buck didn't have to think long about his answer. "You got your guide, Mr. Dorsky. When do we leave?"

"I was thinking in the morning would be soon enough," Dorsky said with a smile.

Chapter 7

The town hall meeting, which had been postponed when the tornado hit, was held a week later at 7:00 p.m. in the Tuttle Saloon. Richard Tuttle had agreed to close down business for the evening in order to host the session. Most of the people owning businesses were there, as well as a few cowboys, ladies of the evening, and traveling salesmen. The issue before them was whether the county should issue $200,000 in bonds to build a rail spur from Newton to Wichita.

"I have assurances from the Santa Fe Railroad that they would assist in laying the track, but the county must pay for it. We citizens have therefore formed the Wichita and Southwestern Railroad Company to accomplish this goal." The speaker was Charles Wringer, a slim middle-aged man with balding head and a gray mustache. "It is imperative for the prosperity of Wichita, and therefore the county, that these bonds be approved."

"Well, now I ain't so sure about that," said Ardmore Grisham, the owner of the Sunset Saloon. "Buildin' a spur down to Wichita would be good for Wichita folk, but it would seriously hurt us in Newton. Look at all the business we would lose if the cattle trade went down there instead of here."

"That might be the best thing that ever happened to Newton," Doc Kern said. Doc was the newly arrived doctor in town, although some doubted he was really a doctor. He was a small man, walked with a limp, and had a sharp face and hawk nose. He claimed to have been a doctor in the late War Between the States, but some said he had only been an orderly. At any rate, he seemed to have some experience and was the only medical man available in the small town.

"Doesn't seem right that we in Newton would have to pay for something that will benefit Wichita and hurt us," Tony Albright, the village blacksmith, said.

"You need to look at the county as a whole," Charles replied, "not just from your own community viewpoint. And anyway, in the long run, it is not an expense but an investment. I'm sure the county will realize a nice return on these bonds."

"Seems to me the county commissioners down in Wichita hardly know we exist up here in Newton," someone said from the back of the room. "Don't know that we would ever benefit from any profit the county makes."

Wally Tomney, not a very tall man, climbed on a table so he could more easily be heard. "Folks, I think we've hit on a key issue here. In my humble opinion, I think it is time that we start thinking seriously about breaking away from Sedgwick and forming our own county." Tomney was with the Sedgwick County Probate Judge's office, living in Newton. He was a rotund man, wore reading glasses usually pushed down to the end of his small nose, had a shaggy bush of white hair on top of his head, and his cheeks were a shiny red, indicating a close relationship with Kentucky whiskey. "It is only common sense that the commissioners, most of whom live in Wichita, would be concerned primarily with their own community and would act accordingly. We who live to the north will never be foremost in their thoughts and their plans."

This was met with a low murmur of approval from the crowd.

Ted Baker was one who concurred with the idea. He was standing at the back of the room watching the discussions. Just then Jenny Johnson walked in and joined them.

"Have I missed anything important?" she asked.

"No, not really," Ted replied. "More talk about forming our own county. How's the new post office coming?" Ted had seen very little of Jenny in the past week. She had joined the rest of the construction gang repairing the building that had been destroyed by the tornado. He had seen her once or twice on the roof, hammer in hand, pounding away at nails. Not a role normally cut out for a woman.

"Moving real fast. We're almost done. Should be able to open next week."

"I see you are adding living quarters at the back. Do you plan to move out of Molly's Rooming House and take up residence there?"

"I do, sometime next week. Trains are starting to come in at all hours, and it will be a lot easier to take in mail bags if I live right there."

"This talk about forming our own county will have to wait for another day." The speaker was Thomas Lane, the owner of the Kansas Hotel and the one who had organized the meeting tonight. "Lots to think about. We'd need to come up with a passel of new offices. County Attorney, Commissioners, County Clerk, Register of Deeds just to name a few. Wouldn't be an easy undertaking. In the meantime, we got this bond election coming up. My main concern is that everything goes off without any disturbances. We'll close down the saloons during voting hours. We don't want any wild Texans who have had a little too much to drink shooting up the place."

"Better hire some law enforcement people then," a voice from the back of the room said.

"Exactly my thoughts," Thomas replied. "I've been giving this some consideration and have a suggestion on who to hire. Some of you might not think they're good choices, but this is a rough town, and we need someone just as rough to keep the peace."

"Who you got in mind?" Doc Kern said.

"Well, I thought we ought to get a cowhand for one and someone from the saloon side for another. I'm thinking Bill Bailey, who most of you know. Runs the holding pens for the cattle. And Mike McCluskie for the other. He's a familiar figure in all the bars and a night watchman for the railroad."

"You got it right about them being rough," Judge R.W.P. Muse, manager of the Santa Fe Land Office, said. "Rumor has it that both of these gentlemen have killed four or five people each over the past few years."

"Better to have them with us than against us," said Zeb Turner, the manager of the railroad office in Newton.

"People, people," Wally Tomney said, holding his pudgy arms up for quiet. "Let us not be too hasty. What do we know about the character of these two persons?"

This was met with raucous laughter from the crowd.

Just then Pedro came into the room, looking somewhat distressed. He spotted Ted and hurried to his side. "Senor," he said, "there is a woman at the depot who is very unhappy."

"An unhappy woman?" Ted said with a chuckle, glancing at Jenny. "Now why would any woman be unhappy in our little paradise?"

"I think, senor, because she thought you would be there to meet her."

Ted's smile evaporated. "Me? Why would she think I would be meeting her?"

"I think maybe, Senor Ted, she is the woman you wish to marry."

Ted stared at Pedro for a full minute trying to digest this news. "Linda," he said finally. "Could it be Linda?"

He rushed from the saloon, Pedro and Jenny right behind him.

The Kansas sky to the west was a brilliant shade of orange, colored by the setting sun. A few clouds drifted slowly to the east, the tops turning to a deep purple as the sun's rays struck them from below. Earlier there had been a light shower, and everything smelled fresh and clean.

Katrina's parents, Anna and Martin Dorsky, and Boris Knopner were in deep conversation around the campfire, speaking rapidly in German. Buck had asked how it was that they spoke German rather than Russian, and Katrina had explained that they had come from Germany before moving to Russia, and German was still their native tongue. Katrina said they were discussing the land they had seen today and what it would mean to their many friends back in Russia. The men had brought along two shovels and at various places on their journey had stopped to dig holes to test the composition of the ground. Mr. Dorsky had explained to Buck, "The land is very good. Two to ten feet of topsoil that has gypsum and lime, making it very porous." Buck didn't know about all of that but figured these two gentlemen knew what they were talking about.

Buck and Katrina sat on a log near their campsite, enjoying the quiet and peaceful evening. Neither felt the need to break the magical silence of the moment by speaking. As they watched, a large quail suddenly appeared on a boulder to their right, looking suspiciously at the clearing in front of him. A few seconds later a female poked her head from a bush near the boulder, followed by six babies. As they crossed the open space in front of Buck and Katrina, the male kept a vigilant watch, not relaxing until his little family had disappeared in the grass to their left. Then he hopped down and scurried after them.

"What was the bird?" Katrina asked. "The husband, he seems very protective for his family."

"Those were quail," Buck said. "Sometimes called bobwhites."

"I believe the man quail makes the good husband. He is looking out for his family and is there with them. Not like the cowboy, I think," she added with a mischievous twinkle in her eyes, "who has the wife and children and then climbs on his horse and goes away and is gone for many months."

"You may have something there," Buck said. "Probably a cowboy would make a bad husband."

"You agree? You do not make the argument?" she said with some surprise.

"Katy, I—do you mind if I call you Katy for short? Katrina sounds so formal."

"I do not mind Katy. It sounds—how you say—okay."

"Katy, I've been doing a lot of thinking on this trip. I've figured it was time I set my sights on something more meaningful then chasing cows, and talking with your dad and Mr. Knopner has decided me. I'm going to take up farming."

"You—a farmer? But what does the cowboy know about farming? You can't just one day say, 'I am a farmer.' There is much to know about the land, the weather, and the seed. I don't think you can say 'I'm a farmer' so easily."

"I've been a farmer for more years than I ever was a cowboy. I grew up on a farm in Illinois. Farming was all I ever knew for the first eighteen years of my life. I've only been a cowboy for a little over three years. Talking with your folks has got me all excited about trying to grow things again. Here in Kansas they plant mostly corn and cotton. Wheat doesn't do too good. The spring wheat—where the seed is planted in the spring—takes too long to mature and suffers from the hot, dry weather we have. And the winter wheat we have now, which is planted in the fall and blooms in the spring, has a soft kernel that gets hit hard by the freezing weather. But your dad has been telling me about a hard winter wheat they have in your country. Plant it in the fall and the hard grain survives the freezing winter then is set to grow when the weather turns nice. You can harvest it in July or August. And he says the land and weather here are almost identical to your home. They plan to bring this wheat to Kansas and make this a big wheat state."

"But you need the land to be a farmer. Where will you get this land?"

"When my dad and mom were…when they died, I lost all interest in farming. Didn't have any kin around, and I couldn't see tying myself down to the farm. Guess I wanted to see something of the rest of the world. And I had another reason. Anyway, I sold the farm and came west. I still have the money from the farm, and out here I can buy three times as much land with it as I owned back there."

"You say there is another reason you sold the farm. What is that?"

Buck hesitated before answering. "My parents were killed by some transients passing through heading west. I had this wild idea that I might be able to find them. Didn't work out, though."

"Oh, Buck. I am so sorry. And what would you do if you were to find these men?"

Buck's face hardened, and his jaw set in a determined expression. "I'd kill them," he said simply.

Katrina was silent for a moment, and then she said, "That is not good. You do the violence, and this leads to more violence. This is a matter for the law I think."

"Law? What law? Have you seen any sheriffs or marshals running around? Out here a man pretty much makes his own law. If you don't stand up for your rights, there are plenty who are just waiting to take them away from you."

"But surely—"

"I know you and your family don't believe in conflict. I don't either. But just saying that doesn't make it go away. It's all around us. Sure, the law would be great if we had any. But even then what law would convict a man just on my say so without any hard evidence? Some things you just got to handle yourself."

"Do you not think the world would be better off if there was no violence in it?"

"Sure. That would be a great place to live in. But just wishing for it doesn't make it happen."

"We know that just because we take the vow of nonviolence it does not go away. But if we would like to live in a world where all men are peaceful, it must start somewhere. For my family, it starts with us. If we say we will not use physical force to settle problems, maybe somebody else will think, 'Hey, this is a good thing,' and the idea will spread. But we cannot answer for everyone. Only for ourselves."

"I'm sorry, Katy. If I ever ran across the men that killed my ma and pa, I know what I would have to do."

"That is not good. I do not think I could live with such a man."

The rest of the evening was spent in moody silence.

Linda Samuels sat on the bench outside of the railroad station in the dim evening light with a mixture of emotions ranging from doubt, confusion, and anger. Where in the world was Ted? What would she do if he didn't show up? How could he do this to her?

She was an attractive woman with golden hair that fell gently to her shoulders, a finely chiseled face accenting blue eyes and full, red lips, which at the moment were pressed in a tight line.

Then from around the corner of the station he appeared, followed closely by a Mexican and a girl.

"Ted Baker," she exclaimed. "I thought you were never going to get here. Where have you been?"

"Linda," he replied. "Is that really you? Where did you come from? Why are you here?"

"Why am I here? I came for that visit that you have been wanting me to make. Didn't you get my letter?"

"Letter?" Suddenly Ted remembered the letter that he had lost during the tornado last week. "Oh my God," he exclaimed. "I did have a letter from you, but I lost it in the wind."

Linda glared at him suspiciously. "You lost it in the wind?"

"Uh…yes…that is…it was a tornado. It tore the roof off the post office and I guess ripped the letter right out of my hands before I could read it."

Linda stared at him for a full minute and then started laughing. "Ted Baker. That is the most ridiculous story I have ever heard. It is so ridiculous that I am halfway inclined to believe that it is true."

Ted felt a great sense of relief. "It really is the truth. But anyway, welcome to Newton. I am glad to see you, Linda—even though surprised."

Ted reached out, pulled her to him, and gave her a long, lingering kiss.

When they broke, Linda looked over Ted's shoulder, seeing a Mexican grinning from ear to ear. Ted looked back and then said, "Linda, I would like for you to meet my two best friends here in Newton. Pedro Lopez, who is my right-hand man at the bakery, and Jenny Johnson, our postmistress. Jenny is the one I badger every day looking for your letters."

"I'm very happy to meet you, Mr. Lopez," Linda said. And a little less warmly, thinking to herself that she hoped that the letters were all he was badgering this girl about, "And you also, Jenny."

"Well, let's get you settled," Ted said. "Is one of those bags yours?" He pointed to three suitcases standing by the bench.

"Darling," Linda said, "they're all mine. You don't think I could travel someplace for a week with only one bag, do you?"

"But, senor," Pedro said, "where do you propose to go? The hotel, she is filled up. The salesmen are sleeping in the lobby. I think there are no rooms in Newton."

"Pedro is right," Jenny said. "None of the boarding houses have any vacancies."

"I have a room at a men's home," Ted said. "Couldn't put you in there."

After a minute, Jenny said, "Ted, she can have my room at Molly's. I'll move into the post office. I was going to move next week anyway."

"Jenny, are you sure? The post office isn't done yet."

"I've got a cot in there. I'll manage okay."

"But you were saying earlier today that you don't have a lock on the door yet."

"No, but I've got my dad's Colt 45, and I know how to use it. I don't think anybody will bother me."

Ted hesitated, not wanting to impose on Jenny, but he could see no alternative. Finally he said, "Jenny, you are an angel."

Jenny found herself blushing, and turned away so neither Ted nor Linda would see. She said, "You and Pedro bring her bags over to Molly's. I'll scoot on over and pack up my things. You can help me move after Linda gets settled." And she hurried off.

Linda, who had been silent during this exchange, said, "She is very nice. She must think very highly of you. I am sorry to be such a bother."

"You are no bother, Linda." He took her arm, gave her a broad smile, and said, "Come on. We'd better get moving before she changes her mind."

Chapter 8

The next day Ted took off work early, turning the bakery over to Pedro, and joined Linda at Molly's. After lunch at the Kansas Hotel, he walked her through the town, pointing out all of the new buildings.

"The town is growing so fast I can hardly keep track of it," Ted said. "Several new law offices have opened just in the last week, and a new food store at the north end of town. It is an exciting time."

"But it is such a dirty place," Linda said. "There are no paved streets, and dust is everywhere. Not like St. Louis. And what do you do for entertainment?"

"Well, you can always hang out in the saloons and wait for the next shooting," Ted joked.

"That's another thing. You never told me what a violent town this is. From what I here at Molly's, there must be someone killed every week."

"Oh, it's not nearly that bad," Ted said. "Sure, we get some cowboys who want to live it up after being on the trail for several months, but most of them are pretty decent folk when they're sober. The worst ones for my money are the people that prey on them. The saloons, gamblers, and prostitutes."

"But it seems quiet now. Very few people are moving about." They were walking on the boardwalk in the part of town known as Hyde Park, where all of the saloons and dance halls were located.

"It's election day. The saloons are closed until six tonight, or else I wouldn't be bringing you down here. It's quiet now, but I suspect things will pick up quickly about then."

"What is the election about? It seems an odd time of the year to be electing people to office."

"Not people, bonds. Folks down in Wichita want to build a railroad spur from Newton down to their place. They've formed a company, and the county wants to sell bonds to raise money for the project. Most of the people up here are against it. Afraid it will take all their business away."

"Newton and Wichita are both in the same county?"

"Yup. There's some agitation to split and form our own county, though."

A cowboy came down the street, wearing a gun slung low on his right leg.

"And another thing," Linda continued. "Everyone here seems to think it necessary to carry a gun. No wonder there is so much violence. Even your Jenny has a pistol—what did she say, a Colt .44."

Ted grimaced. "She's not *my* Jenny," he said, although he wondered a little about it even as he spoke. He did feel protective toward her.

"Look at this cowboy coming toward us now. He's got a gun swinging at his side. And look at what a mean look he has in his eyes. Not like the men in Illinois."

"Matter of fact, he is an Illinois man," Ted said, recognizing Buck McNurty. "He comes from Sweetwater, the little home town we grew up in. Maybe you remember him. Buck McNurty."

"McNurty? The cute little farm boy who lived south of town?"

"One and the same," Ted said "Hey, Buck, come on over here and say hello to one of your old flames. Linda Samuels."

"By golly, I'd recognize you anywhere," Buck said as he approached the two. "Though you've gotten even prettier than I remember you."

They chatted on the boardwalk for a while, when Ted said, "Buck, you seem a little down at the mouth. Didn't my donuts go over so well?"

"Oh, they were great. Got the job, but it was a mixed blessing. The good news is that I've finally decided what I want to do with my life. I'm going to become a farmer again. Looking into buying some land over to the northeast, up by Walton."

"A farmer?" Ted said. "That's great. But what's the bad news?"

"Well, there's this girl I'm kinda sweet on. A Mennonite from Russia. I guess we have a little difference of opinion about how sometimes you have to settle your own arguments. Mennonites are against any kind of violence, you know. Anyway, that's kinda come up between us, and I'm not sure how to get around it."

"I'm sure you will find a way, Buck," Linda said. "Although I might be inclined to take her side on this one."

"What are you going to grow, Buck?" Ted asked. "Corn?"

"Mostly corn to start with," Buck replied. "But I hope someday to get some of that hard winter wheat I hear they have in Russia that the Mennonites keep talking about. They think it would do great here in Kansas."

"That would sure help my business," Ted said. "I use the soft wheat for donuts and pastries, but the hard wheat does much better in making bread."

———————

At the far end of the street, Mike McCluskie emerged from the Dew Drop Inn, Jim Riley walking along beside him.

"It's almost three, Mr. McCluskie," Jim said. "No trouble so far. I guess all those cowboys know better than to raise a ruckus when you're on the job."

Mike McCluskie and Bill Bailey had been hired by the county to keep the peace during the election. They had both been patrolling the town, careful to keep out of each other's way.

"Actually I'm a little disappointed," McCluskie said. "I was looking forward to a little action today."

Riley was looking pale and thinner than ever. He had been in bed for the previous day and a half with a fever and nonstop coughing but now was feeling a little better. As they were passing the Silver Streak Saloon, they heard a loud voice shouting inside.

"Maybe we get to earn our keep after all, Jim," McCluskie said, and he turned into the building. A cowboy was at the bar arguing with the proprietor.

"You been closed all day," the puncher was saying. "There's been plenty of time for anyone to vote who wants to, and I got a thirst that's downright terrible. I say we open up this here bar right now." He pulled his pistol from its holster and laid it on the bar. "What do you say, pardner?" he said to the bartender in a menacing voice.

McCluskie stepped up behind him. "You got a problem, cowboy?"

The Texan turned, sized up McCluskie, and said, "We're just gettin' ready to open this saloon, mister. You got any objections?"

"Matter of fact, I do. We have an election going on, and the bars are closed till six. I suggest you satisfy your thirst with a little water from our town well until then."

"Water? The thirst I got ain't going to be satisfied by any old water. I need me some whiskey."

"Cowboy, I'll tell you this only once. Get out of this saloon and stop pestering the barkeeper."

"Say, who do you think you are? I got a right to be wherever I want to be."

McCluskie pulled his gun and slashed it across the cowboy's face, the gun sight leaving a jagged cut that started to bleed profusely.

"Now get out." He picked up the gun from the counter and stuck it in his belt. "I'll just hang on to this."

The cowhand pulled a bandana from the back of his neck, held it to his bleeding cheek, and stumbled out of the door into the street, just as Linda, Ted, and Buck were passing. He brushed against Linda slightly, getting a splotch of blood on her dress.

Linda gave a shriek and jumped back. "Oh, Ted," she cried. "Did you see that man? And look at my dress. It's got blood on it. It's ruined!"

Buck recognized the man as one of the cowhands who worked at the cow pens. "What happened, Butch?" he asked.

Butch replied, "Some man in there. He's crazy. Hit me with his pistol for no reason."

Ted watched the man stagger down the street and then turned back to Linda. "Sorry about that, honey. I guess we shouldn't have come down to this part of town. But it's just a little blood. It will wash out okay."

Linda was bordering on hysteria. "Wash out? Do you think I'll ever wear this dress again? Dear God, look at it. And that man. Who could have done that to him?"

McCluskie and Jim Riley came out of the saloon. McCluskie looked at Linda, smiled, tipped his hat, and walked on down the street.

"Ted, you've got to take me back to the rooming house. This dress is ruined, and I've got to get into something else." She stared down at the smudge of blood and shivered.

As they headed out of the Hyde Park area and crossed the tracks into the more legitimate part of town, they passed the Kansas Hotel and noticed several people leaving with traveling bags. On an impulse, Ted said, "You know, there just might be a vacancy at the hotel. If there is, would you rather stay there than at the rooming house?"

"Are you kidding?" Linda replied. "There is almost no privacy at Molly's. And besides, I don't like feeling indebted to your post office friend."

They checked at the front desk, and the clerk told them they were in luck. They had a room Linda could have that would be ready in about forty-five minutes. The rest of the afternoon was spent in getting Linda packed up and moved into her new quarters.

––––––––––––––––––

At six, Hyde Park came to life. The bars were open, the honky-tonk pianos were pounding away, the prostitutes were decked out in colorful dresses, and the whiskey was in abundance.

McCluskie walked down the street and turned in at Tuttle's Saloon, his sidekick, Riley, right behind him. He stopped just inside the door, looked around, and started for a table in the back of the room when Bill Bailey stepped in front of him.

"Just a minute, McCluskie. I got a bone to pick with you. I heard you pistol whipped one of my cowboys this afternoon for no good reason."

"Oh, there was reason enough," McCluskie replied. "He was disturbing the peace. I'd have arrested him if we had a jail to put him in, but we don't, so I had to settle him down the old-fashioned way. While we're talking, Bailey, I heard it said that you been trying to get friendly with my woman, Rosie Williams. I'm telling you straight up to stay away from her."

"McCluskie, you're nothing but a low-life scoundrel that would beat his own mother to death just for the pleasure of it." With that, Bailey swung a hard right fist into the groin of McCluskie and followed with a left to the jaw. McCluskie went down but rose with a cruel smile spreading across his face. "Bailey, I been waiting for you to do something like that. Now we'll settle this thing once and for all." He went in swinging, and Bailey caught one square on his nose, which started bleeding profusely. The two men struggled against each other for the next three minutes, each going down at least once, but McCluskie was slowly getting the best of it.

A crowd gathered around, cheering them on. Both men were bloody and breathing hard when McCluskie connected with an uppercut that sent Bailey back through the doors of the saloon and onto the boardwalk. As Bailey tried to regain his feet, McCluskie struck again, sending Bailey sprawling into the street.

Both men were gasping for air, Bailey lying on one elbow in the street and McCluskie leaning against a post on the porch. Suddenly McCluskie pulled his gun and shot Bailey in the chest. He then walked over to Bailey and fired three more times.

The cheering crowd fell into a shocked silence. Finally one of the spectators said in a low voice, "That was out and out murder."

McCluskie swung around to face the man. "What do you mean? He was going for his gun. This man's a known killer. Shot at least half a dozen men. I fired in self-defense."

Another in the crowd said, "I didn't see him grabbing for any iron. And why did you have to go shoot him three more times?"

"He was shot in the lungs," McCluskie said. "I didn't want to see him die a slow, hurtful death. I did him a favor."

Someone else spoke out, "McCluskie's right. Bailey was reaching for his gun sure as I'm standing here."

"Looked to me like cold-blooded killing," yet another said.

There was a growing murmur among the crowd, some arguing that the shooting was justified and others that it was not, but the latter seemed to be in the majority. McCluskie looked around, not liking the tone of those assembled in the street. He spotted Jim Riley standing nearby and walked over to him.

"Jim, there seems to be some dispute about what just happened. You saw him go for his pistol, didn't you?"

"Yes, sir. He was aiming to shoot you right enough. You did what you had to do."

"It was self-defense, pure and simple. But I'll have a hard time convincing the cowpokes of that. I'm thinking that I should clear out of here for a few days and see how things shape up. And knowing these cow chasers, there just might be some that would come gunning for me. Think I'll take the night train up to Florence till things cool down a bit. I'd appreciate it if you monitored things down here and kept me appraised."

McCluskie shouldered his way through the crowd, went to his room, cleaned up, and packed a few things. He left the hotel by the back door and headed to the depot.

CHAPTER 9

I t was a bright, sunny Kansas morning with a gentle western breeze cooling the dusty streets of Newton. Even in town the meadowlarks could be heard singing in the countryside, sounding like a dozen musicians playing on their flutes.

Inside Ted's bakery, the customers sitting at four tables were enjoying various pastries, fresh out of the oven, along with steaming black coffee. It had become a popular place for the locals to gather and find out all of the latest in the town's happenings.

Sitting at one of the tables was Wally Tomney who was expounding on the current political situation. Although he was ostensibly talking to the two gentlemen sitting at the table with him, he spoke in a loud voice and frequently looked around the room to include everyone within earshot—people at the other tables and customers coming and going.

"What this town needs to do is to get serious about splitting from Sedgwick County and forming our own government. Sedgwick County is Wichita, and Wichita is Sedgwick County. All of the county revenues are being spent for improvements down there. How much money have you seen flow into Newton for better roads or new bridges? And now they've passed that bond issue, by only four hundred and forty votes mind you, to build a railway spur down to their city at the county's expense. That will seriously hurt our economy."

The two gentlemen who were with him nodded in agreement.

"And another thing," Tomney continued, "we need law and order in this county. It is shameful how much gunplay goes on without any restraint. I tell you this town is not safe for our women and children."

"How about you, Wally," Ted said from behind the counter, "are you willing to pay a city tax to hire a town marshal?"

"You'd better believe it, son. This place is not just a wide spot in the road. We're a community, and it's time we started acting like one."

Just then Ray Kennedy, the federal marshal who lived in Wichita, walked in and strode up to the counter. "My wife has told me that I'm not to return home without a loaf of that sourdough bread we've been hearing so much about. Matter of fact, better make it two loaves."

"Marshal Kennedy," Tomney said in a loud voice, "have you arrested McCluskie yet for that blatant shooting on our streets last week?"

Kennedy turned and stared hard at Tomney. Finally he said, "I've looked into the killing. Talked with a lot of witnesses. Seems to me it is a clear case of self-defense."

Tomney laughed. "That's not exactly the way most of us feel, Marshal. Everyone I've talked with says it was out and out murder."

"Well, you've obviously only talked with half of the witnesses. Those that were there are equally divided in what they think they saw. So if you can't go by witnesses, you have to apply a little logic to the case. There had been a pretty rough brawl, and one of the participants won and one lost. Now in that situation, which of the two would be most likely to pull a gun? The winner, who had just demonstrated that he was the better man, or the loser, who had lost face and was a mighty upset with losing? I think the answer is obvious. The loser made the play. Clearly a case of self-defense."

The marshal paid for his two loaves of bread and, with a challenging look at Tomney, walked out of the shop. Tomney said nothing, and shortly afterward he and his friends also left.

Linda Samuels was sitting at one of the tables, and now with a lull in business, Ted came over and sat down beside her. "What do you think of our little town, Linda? A lot of exciting things going on."

"Oh, Ted. This place is awful. Half of the town is made up of saloons and gambling halls and women of loose virtue. And people are shot in the streets almost every day by those…those awful cowboys. How can you see anything good about your Newton?"

"Linda, I know we are rough around the edges right now. But that will change. I think this town has a great future."

"As a cow town? A dirty, dusty cow town?"

"No, not as a cow town. Newton is a railroad town. This is a main link on the Santa Fe Railroad, a place where crews will change out and repairs made to engines and cars, and corporate offices will be located. And before long it won't be cattle on the rails. It'll be people and farm produce. This will be a great farming community. People like Buck McNurty buying land and looking to agriculture. That's the future of this town. And I want to be a part of it, Linda. Doesn't that sound exciting to you at all?"

"I'll never in my whole life understand how you can be so worked up over a place like this when you could be living in St. Louis. I have hoped that you would get this out of your system and come back home where you belong. Even that gentleman who just left recognized what a dismal place this is."

"Tomney? That bag of wind?"

"I thought he made perfect sense. The first rational person I've met since I arrived here. Including present company, I might add."

"I don't necessarily disagree with anything he said," Ted replied. "In fact, most of it is right on target. It's just that he's such a pompous you-know-what. I think he's already running for office in our growing community."

As they talked, Jenny Johnson came into the shop and, seeing Ted and Linda, came over to the table. "Mind if I join you?" she asked.

"Of course not," Linda replied. "Pull up a chair and have some of Ted's delicious pastries."

"You just missed Wally Tomney expounding on his political views," Ted said. "Pretty interesting stuff."

"That bag of wind?" Jenny said.

Ted laughed, while Linda glared at both of them. "Sounds like you two agree on everything," she said. "Isn't that nice. Makes it easy to be in each other's company, I presume."

Jenny looked embarrassed, and Ted decided to change the topic. "How is the new post office coming along?"

"Almost done," Jenny said, thankful for the diversion. "And I actually have a bed in the living quarters now. All the comforts of home."

"If you ladies will excuse me a moment," Ted said, "I'd better go check on Pedro. Sometimes he leaves the bread in the ovens a little too long."

He rose and walked back to the counter just as Judge Muse came into the store to buy a loaf of sour dough bread.

"Ted, you are a blessing to this community with your bake shop here. This town's about to grow up, and it's going to need young men like yourself. I hope you will take an active roll in community affairs."

"I don't know about that, Judge. I'm not much for politics."

"Precisely why we need you. Just keep an open mind."

The judge nodded to Linda and greeted Jenny as he left. "Keep an eye on this young man, Miss Johnson."

There was an awkward silence between the two women, and finally Jenny said, "I don't know what he meant by that."

"And just who is he?"

"Judge Muse. He's a Civil War hero from what I hear. Also a probate judge. Right now he the commissioner of land sales for the railroad. He's the one that picked the site for our town and is one of the civic leaders." After a slight pause, Jenny said, "Ted tells me that the two of you grew up together back in Illinois."

"Oh, yes. A little town named Sweetwater. I live in St. Louis now."

"I understand Ted's father had a bakery there?"

"Yes. Still does. Ted can be so stubborn. His father wanted Ted to come into business with him. Or if Ted didn't want to do that, he offered to set Ted up in St. Louis. But no, Ted has to prove himself on his own. His father came west to Illinois from New York and was successful, so Ted figures he has to do the same thing. I had hoped he would have this out of his system by now, but he seems as determined as ever. Men can be so pig-headed, don't you think?"

Jenny was saved from responding by Ted's return. At that point, Buck McNurty and Katrina Dorsky rushed into the shop and came over to the table. "Hi, Ted," Buck said. "Don't know if you've ever met Katrina."

Introductions were made while Ted studied Buck's attire. "Couldn't figure out what was wrong," he said. "Now I know. You look almost naked without your gun."

Buck laughed. "I feel almost naked," he said. "But I decided that guns just lead to violence, something I'm dead set against." He stole a sideways glance at Katrina while he said this, noting with pleasure that she smiled broadly at his statement.

"A cowboy friend of Buck has seen the buffalo near here," she said. "We are going to ride the pony out to see them. A buffalo I have never seen."

"Thought we would make a picnic out of it," Buck said. "We need to get some of that famous sourdough bread of yours to take along. If you're free, why don't you and Linda join us?"

"Ride a horse?" Linda said. "Not for me, I'm afraid."

"That sounds like a great idea, Buck," Ted said. "Pedro can handle things here at the shop. We can rent a buggy over at the stable, Linda. It's a great day for a picnic. How about it, Jenny? Would you like to come along?"

"No, thanks," Jenny said, although she would have loved to see the herd. "I've got some things I need to get done at the post office. You all go ahead."

Ted was disappointed, although Linda was secretly pleased.

Later the foursome located the small herd of buffalo in a meadow to the northwest of town. They pulled to within a hundred yards of the animals that seemed unconcerned with their presence.

"What a magnificent beast," Ted said. "First time I've ever seen one."

"I'd guess there's almost fifty of them in this herd," Buck said. "Time was they roamed the country around here in the millions. That was before all the buffalo hunters started killing them off. Not many of the creatures left anymore."

"But they look so ragged," Linda said. "In the pictures I've seen of them, they have such a beautiful coat of brown fur. These poor animals look like they have leprosy—mostly skin and only patches of fur here and there."

"That's because they shed their winter coats in the summer," Buck said. "They'll grow a new one this fall."

They watched the herd grazing in the grass for almost an hour while they ate the sandwiches Katrina had prepared. The sun was low in the west and the shadows long before they started back to Newton.

"This is a beautiful evening," Linda said. "Maybe there is something to be said for this part of the country after all."

Buck gazed at her as they rode toward town. *She is beautiful*, he thought, *and as Buck said the other day, I am a lucky man. Very lucky.*

Chapter 10

Mike McCluskie returned to Newton as soon as he heard that he was not a wanted man and on Saturday evening took up his usual position at the poker table in Tuttle's Saloon.

Hugh Anderson, hanging out at the Eldorado Gaming Emporium, was furious. "That murdering no-good skunk. Sitting down there playing cards big as life, while Bill Bailey lies in his grave. Someone should go down there right now and blow his head off," he fumed.

By that night Hugh had worked himself into a near frenzy, saying that he was personally going to kill McCluskie before another sun came up in the east. Bill Bailey had been a good man and a good friend, and what were friends for if they didn't stand up for each other?

Curly Martin and Gramps Thompson were in the crowd at the Eldorado and became alarmed as Hugh became more and more bellicose. They didn't want to see Hugh get himself into trouble with the law.

"Hugh," Curly said, "you've been a good friend and a decent man to work for, and I sure don't want to see you do anything you'd be sorry about. Man like McCluskie, he's going to get his just rewards someday from someone, but it don't need to be you getting crosswise with the marshal. Just let him be."

"He'll get his reward all right," Hugh said, "and I'm the man that's going to give it to him. Bill Bailey was a friend of mine, and I owe him. I've never let another man do my chores for me, and I don't plan to start now."

Curly saw that there was no use in trying to talk Anderson out of confronting McCluskie and decided that maybe he could convince McCluskie to leave town again before that happened. He and Gramps left the Eldorado and headed down to Tuttle's.

The place was packed with cowboys, railroad laborers, gamblers, and women of the evening. Curly paused at the door looking over the noisy, crowded room and finally spotted McCluskie sitting at a table near the faro wheel with his shadow, Jim Riley. Gramps sauntered over to the bar while Curly walked up to McCluskie's table.

"Hi, Mike," Curly said. "Mind if I join you?"

McCluskie looked at him suspiciously. "Something on your mind? Go ahead. Pull up a chair."

Curly sat down at the table. "McCluskie, I sure don't have any great liking for you, but I reckon you should be warned. Hugh Anderson, down at the Eldorado, is getting pretty worked up over your shooting of Bill Bailey. If I were you, I think I'd be letting the dust settle from a rather hasty exit from this here town. And I don't mean tomorrow. I mean right now."

"Sonny, I take that as a well-meaning bit of advice, but if Hugh Anderson has anything to say to me, he can say it to my face. He doesn't need to send any of his cow-chasing friends like yourself to do it for him."

Curly sat for a moment studying the gambler and then turned to Jim Riley. "If you are a friend to this man, Riley, you'll tell him for his own good that he ought to take a little vacation from this town. Vamoose, while he still can."

"Mr. McCluskie is quite capable of making up his own mind and handling his own affairs," Riley replied. "I think this Anderson might be the one that should be thinking of getting out of town."

Curly turned back to McCluskie. "Have it your way. I just thought I might save some of your blood from spilling on the floor here. Just don't tell me you weren't warned." He got up and joined Gramps at the bar.

"Have any luck with him?" Gramps asked.

"No. I don't like it. I sure hope Anderson cools down some before he does something stupid."

McCluskie pulled a Colt .44 from his holster as soon as Curly left and laid it on the table beside his cards where he could get at it quickly.

As the evening progressed, the crowds became bigger and nosier. At one in the morning, the cowboys, railroad workers, and gamblers were in high gear all across Hyde Park.

At the Eldorado, John Shelton, the proprietor, announced in a loud voice, "One o'clock, boys. The bar is closing. Everyone can finish their drink, and then this establishment will be closed for the night."

There was a general murmur of dissent from the crowd. "You can't close now," someone called out. "The party's just getting in high gear."

"Sorry, men. It's Sunday morning, and if we don't close, we'll have the good folk of this community coming down on us for sure. Drink up. We'll open again Monday morning at eight."

Hugh Anderson was at a table in the back of the room with three others. To his right was Billy Garrett, a tall, thin cowboy from Texas. Sitting across the pine table was Henry Kearnes, also from Texas and also thin but a good deal shorter. To his left was Jim Wilkerson, a short, chubby fellow from Kentucky who now called himself a Texan.

"Well, boys," Hugh said, "it's time to put action to where my words are. Henry here was just down at Tuttle's. McCluskie is still there. Seems Tuttle has sent the band home but is keeping the bar open a little longer for the crowd."

"Hugh, you'd best get the drop on him," Billy said. "I've seen McCluskie with a gun, and that man is fast. Don't go giving him an even chance, or he'll beat you to the draw sure as I'm sitting here."

"It's not going to be fair, Billy, and it's not going to be pretty. I'm going in with gun in hand, and I'll shoot him where he sits. Same kind of chance he gave Bill Bailey."

"Can't make it too obvious or you'll have the law after you," Jim Wilkerson said. "I got myself an idea. Why don't Henry and Billy and myself meander on down there, and when you brace McCluskie, we'll start shooting up the place. That'll make everyone duck and will fill the place with gun smoke. You kill McCluskie, and nobody will notice who started what, and we'll swear afterward that it was McCluskie who drew first."

Hugh considered the idea and then shook his head. "I don't want to get you boys involved in my fight. I'll take my chances with the law."

"It's not your fight alone, Hugh," Billy said. "We all liked Bailey. He was one of us. We got a stake in this too. And I don't see as how you have any say-so about it. We're off to Tuttle's now. You can follow when you're ready."

The other two nodded in agreement, and the three of them got up and headed for the door.

Curly, seeing Billy, Henry, and Jim enter Tuttle's Saloon and spread out among the crowd, knew something was up. He made his way over to Billy and asked, "What's happening, Billy? Hugh isn't going to do anything foolish, is he?"

"Nah, Curly. Nothing foolish. But best you stay out of it just the same."

Hugh Anderson finished his drink and headed out of the door of the El Dorado. Outside he took a deep breath, savoring the cool night air, and glanced up at a full moon. *A good night to make things right*, he thought. He pulled his six-shooter from its holster and checked the chambers to make sure it was fully loaded. Then he pulled his hat low over his forehead and started for Tuttle's Saloon, the pistol still in his hand.

When he got there, he paused a moment then entered through the swinging doors. He surveyed the crowd, spotting McCluskie sitting at a table calmly playing a game of solitaire. *That son of a coyote, sitting there like he owns the world*, he thought. It was almost more than he could take.

Curly spotted Hugh by the door and pushed through the noisy crowd, trying to reach him, but he was too late.

Hugh walked up to McCluskie and through clenched teeth barked out, "You are a cowardly cross-eyed snake, and I will blow the top of your head off." He raised his pistol to fire as McCluskie grabbed his own gun and aimed at Hugh.

At that instant, Billy, Henry, and Jim pulled their pistols and, yelling loudly, fired into the ceiling. The distraction caused McCluskie to jerk his hand slightly, and his shot missed Anderson, but Hugh's bullet plowed into McCluskie's chest. McCluskie fell out of his chair but managed to get another shot off, hitting Hugh in the leg. The other three cowboys kept shooting into the air, emptying their guns, while Hugh, with blood running down his leg, hobbled over to McCluskie and shot him three more times as he lay on the floor.

Jim Riley stood at the table, watching in disbelief as McCluskie was shot down. The saloon was filled with gun smoke, cutting visibility considerably. The shooting ended as abruptly as it started, and an eerie silence fell over the crowd as they started to get up from the floor and looked around to see what had happened. Anderson stumbled into a chair and tried to stop the flow of blood in his leg.

Riley stood in shocked silence, tears coming in his eyes. His idol and protector was dead, killed by these cowboys. After a minute, he walked to the front door, pulled out both of his pistols, and muttered, "Mr. McCluskie was my friend. I ride for the brand." He blasted away with both guns at the group of cowboys that had gathered around McCluskie's body. His aim was fairly accurate with his right hand, but his left arm was shaking badly, and the bullets went everywhere.

The first shot from his right hand hit Henry Kearnes squarely in the chest, while his left-handed missile struck an innocent railroad man standing at the bar by the name of Patrick Lee. He would die from his wounds.

Riley continued firing both guns till they clicked on empty.

Curly Martin, who had tried to avert the gun-pay, caught one of the early bullets in the neck. He staggered through the front door into the street and collapsed and died on the steps of Krum's Dance Hall across the street. Henry Kearnes was mortally wounded but would hold on for a week before giving up the ghost. Billy Garrett was hit in the chest and shoulder and would die within the hour. Jim Wilkerson was shot in the nose and leg but would recover. Hugh Anderson, sitting in a chair with his leg wound from McCluskie, was not hit. Another railroad man, Josh Hickey, was shot in the calf. In all, Riley mortally wounded three cowboys and one railroad man and wounded three others.

Again an unnatural quiet descended on the saloon, now filled with the acid sting of smoke from the guns.

Riley holstered his two weapons, looked around the saloon at the dead and wounded, and walked out through the back door.

CHAPTER 11

T he news of the shooting spread quickly throughout Newton. Ted's Bakery saw an early morning increase in citizens who were questioning, confused, and angry over the events of only a few hours previous.

Jenny rushed in to the shop, anxious to talk with Ted about the exciting events.

"There is going to be a meeting of the town council at seven," Ted said. "Sure would like to sit in, but I can't leave Pedro alone with all this business."

"Ted, you go on. It's Sunday, and the post office is closed. I can help out here. Pedro will help me if I get in trouble."

Ted gave her a grateful look, took off his apron, and started for the door. He stopped only long enough to give Jenny a quick kiss on the cheek. She turned beet red, and as Ted left, he couldn't help thinking how nice that had felt.

When he arrived at the lobby of the Kansas Hotel, Wally Tomney was speaking, his eye glasses perched on the end of his nose and his white shaggy hair bobbing with each word.

"These Texans have gone too far. I say the sooner the railroad lays track to Wichita, the better. Let all that riffraff end up there instead of here."

"Way I heard it, it wasn't the Texans but some sick kid did all the shooting," said Stanley Fisher, a new lawyer in town.

"That may be, but for my money, it was that gambler McCluskie that started it," said Fred Lehman who had just opened a hardware store in the middle of town. "He's a known killer. Shot a cowboy in cold blood less than a week ago."

The group continued to talk and argue over what had actually happened and who was to blame, when Ray Kennedy, the federal marshal, raised his hand for silence. News of the massacre, as it was being called, had been telegraphed to Wichita, and Kennedy had been informed almost immediately. By three in the morning, he was saddled and on his way to Newton.

"Can I have your attention!" he spoke in a commanding voice. The crowd slowly quieted to listen to what the Marshal had to say. "It's obvious to me that there's a lot of speculation about what did or did not happen, and we need to get at the facts while they are fresh in everyone's mind. I suggest that we form a coroner's jury to look into the matter. Doctor Kern of your community is associated with the County Coroner's Office and so has the authority to convene an investigation into the killings."

"Excellent idea," Tomney said. "I for one would be happy to serve on the inquiry."

"Count me in." Zeb Turner was the manager of the AT&SF railroad office in Newton.

A half dozen others volunteered, including Ted Baker.

The group started hearings at eight.

"I think the first order of business is to select a foreman for the inquiry," Doc Kern said.

"But as coroner, aren't you automatically in charge?" Zeb asked.

"No. I will testify as to the cause of death, but it is not up to me to decide if the death was justified or not. That's the job for all of you, and you will need a jury foreman to guide you in your findings."

"That would make sense," Jacob Fuller, owner of the Pioneer Store, said. "I nominate Ted Baker. He seems like a sensible young man with clear thinking."

"Good choice," echoed Zeb Turner. "I move we name him our leader by acclamation."

"Let's not be too hasty," Tomney said. He obviously would like to be the foreman himself. "Don't you think we should have some discussion on the matter? Mr. Baker is a good man, I'm sure. But what are his qualifications for this particular job?"

"He's qualified. Let's get on with the business at hand," said Jacob. This met with a general round of approval. "Looks like you're it, Ted," he said.

Ted looked around the group. "Okay. I would agree with Mr. Tomney that I am probably not the best person for the job, but I reckon I can serve as a facilitator. Let's get started."

"Which one of the deceased are we supposed to be investigating?" Tony Albright was Newton's blacksmith. "We'll be here for a month if we try to study how each one died and who did it."

"It seems that Mike McCluskie was the first one killed," Ted said. "Everything else followed that first shooting. Let's see if we can figure out just how this whole thing started. That's what we need to know."

Doc Kern began the proceedings by describing the cause of death for McCluskie. "He died from four gunshot wounds to his chest and abdomen," he testified.

One of the first witnesses called was Gramps Thompson.

"Please tell us in your own words exactly what you saw last night, Mr. Thompson," Ted said.

"Well, me and my good friend, Curly Martin, were at Tuttle's having a drink," Gramps said. He was obviously uncomfortable and hesitant to say too much.

"Was there a particular reason for you being there?"

"Reason? Well, it was Saturday night, and every so often on Saturday nights I get a hankering for a drink"

"We have heard, Mr. Thompson, that you came to Tuttle's Bar specifically to warn McCluskie of some possible violence toward him. Is that true?"

Gramps looked around at the group with a desperate look in his eye, as if there might be some way he could sneak out of the room. Finally he said, "There'd been some talk about getting even for McCluskie killing Bill Bailey a week ago. That's the shooting that you ought to be investigatin'. That was out and out murder, and nothing was being done about it."

"And who was it that Curly was warning McCluskie about?"

Gramps looked down at his boots and didn't answer.

"Was it Hugh Anderson?"

Gramps shuffled his feet and finally answered in a low voice, "I reckon." Then he looked up and added, "Maybe it doesn't mean much to all you town folk that a cowboy was shot down in cold blood a week ago, but it matters to us. Hugh Anderson was doing what every red-blooded man wanted to do. When there's no law, you got to right the wrongs on your own."

Later Richard Tuttle was called.

"Yes, I saw Anderson when he came into my saloon. He had a wild look in his eye and was holding a gun at his side. He walked over to McCluskie, hollered that he was going to blow his head off, and started shooting."

Other witnesses pretty much substantiated this version, and by 12:30 p.m. the jury summarized their findings. Mike McCluskie, gambler and night watchman for the railroad, had been shot and killed without provocation by one Hugh Anderson, cowboy from Texas. A warrant for his arrest was issued almost immediately.

The word spread around town quickly, and the Texans were outraged. They felt the killing of McCluskie was entirely justified and that Anderson should be hailed as a hero, not wanted for murder. Added to this was the fact that six of their group had been shot that night, and no one was being charged for that.

Marty Fitzpatrick was one of the wranglers who was stirring up the anger, suggesting that they should hang everyone that had been on the coroner's jury and burn down the whole town.

———————

As soon as the coroner's jury reported their findings to the Marshal, Ted hurried to Linda's room, but she was not there. He came down to the dining area and found her having a late lunch. Sitting with her but not eating was Buck McNurty.

As Ted approached the table, Linda gave him a scorching look. *Good thing I'm not paper*, he thought, *or I'd catch on fire for sure.*

As he sat down, both Linda and Buck started talking at once.

"Whoa," Ted said, "one at a time."

Linda started up again. "Ted Baker, you were going to be here at ten this morning for breakfast with me. I waited all morning, not daring to come down by myself with all this shooting going on. And you know this is the last day of my trip. Oh, Ted, what a terrible town this is. When are you going to give up this wild idea of yours and come back to a civilized place?"

"Linda, I'm sorry. Last night's troubles just took over everything else this morning. I have been on a coroner's jury, and we just now wound everything up."

"That's what I wanted to talk with you about," Buck interjected. "Some of the cowboys are pretty worked up over what is being done to Hugh Anderson. They see him as a wronged man and are threatening to ride into town and hang everyone that was on the jury. Thought I better warn you. Might be a good idea if you took a little vacation for a few days till things calm down."

Linda was shocked by Buck's warning. "You mean they would actually do something like that?"

"It's been known to happen before," Buck said. "I've tried to talk sense into them, and most of them listen, but there's a few that are just plain wild and mean."

"Ted, that settles it," Linda said. "You've got to leave with me first thing in the morning."

"I don't think there's going to be any trouble," Ted said. "The Marshal is here, and he's going to arrest Hugh Anderson. Once that's happened, everybody will calm down."

"I think he's going to have a little trouble if he tries to nab Hugh," Buck said. "He's been wounded, you know, and from what I hear is pretty bad off. But he's got a cadre of cowpunchers taking care of him down at the El Dorado, and I for one sure wouldn't want to try to get him out of there."

As if on cue, the Marshal walked into the dining room along with Carlos King, a deputy sheriff for Sedgwick County. Carlos was a smaller man than the Marshal with a two-day stubble of beard and a long, drooping mustache. He had a wide mouth, which frequently opened in a friendly smile. They sat at one of the tables and studied the menu.

"Hey, Marshal," one of the patrons called out. "Have you arrested Anderson for killing McCluskie yet?"

The Marshal gave him a cool look. "No need right now," he said. "He's been shot and from what I hear is pretty near death. He ain't going anywhere. We'll just let tempers simmer down a bit before jumping into the fish pond."

Buck gave Ted a knowing look. "Sounds like our Marshal has more sense than you'd think."

"How about that kid Riley that did all the shooting?" Ted asked.

"I've been trying to track him down. Seems like he just disappeared into thin air. Nobody's seen him since last night. I'm thinking he might have caught the early train back to Kansas City. From what I hear he's another one, in addition to Anderson, that doesn't have long to live. I guess the good Lord might just settle both accounts for us."

Ted turned his attention back to Buck and Linda. "Buck, did you know any of the cowboys that got shot last night?"

Buck hesitated before answering, a painful look crossing his face. "Knew several of them. One was my best friend. Curly Martin. He tried to stop the shooting. He was trying to be a peacemaker and caught one in the neck for his trouble. Guess God's calling him his son now."

It took Ted a minute to make the connection. *Blessed are the peacemakers, for they shall be called sons of God.*

"Yes, I'm sure God is mighty proud of him," Ted said.

"I'd best be moving on," Buck said. "But be careful. Most of the cowboys are pretty sensible, but there's a few that are looking for a chance to stir up trouble." He rose from the table and left.

"Linda, I'm sorry things turned out so crazy this morning, but we still have this afternoon. There's a place I wanted to show you."

"Ted Baker, I'm not stepping foot out of this hotel till I leave for the train in the morning. This town is not safe." Seeing the disappointment in Ted's face, she relented a little. "Just what is it you wanted me to see?"

"I've started building our home, Linda. Haven't got very far yet, but the foundation is in. It's on east Second Street."

Linda stared at him for a full minute before responding. "Oh, Ted. You are impossible. I can't get out of this town quick enough, and here you're building a house in it. What am I to do with you?"

"You could marry me, I guess."

Linda's attitude softened, and she gave him an affectionate look. "Now that's an idea. Absolutely the best idea I've heard since I got here." After a minute, she sighed and said, "I guess I have to get used to the thought that you can be stubborn when you get some crazy idea in your mind. Just like when you were a little boy. Well, tell me about the house."

Chapter 12

Later in the afternoon Wally Tomney came through the lobby carrying two traveling bags and looking distressed.

"Looks like you are going on a trip, Wally," Ted said.

"You bet I am. And you'd best be heading out, too. Most of us who served on the jury are on our way to friendlier places. Me, I'm going to Florence till things calm down around here."

"You're really not that worried, are you?"

"Ted, did you see any of the notices that have been posted around town? They promise that any of the jurors that haven't left by nightfall will be honored guests at a neck stretching party."

The words brought a worried frown back to Linda's face. "Oh, Ted, you've got to pack up and leave town. Not with me tomorrow but with Mr. Tomney tonight. You have to get out of this dreadful place."

"I'm not leaving, Linda. The jury didn't do anything wrong. We just looked at the facts and declared what was obvious. Nobody is going to hurt anyone for that."

"A very foolish attitude, young man," Tomney said. "Especially for the foreman of our little group."

He tipped his hat to Linda, picked up his suitcases, and hurried out the door on his way to the train station.

Linda couldn't decide whether to be worried about Ted or to be mad at him. He tried to reassure her that nothing was going to happen, but with little success. They spent the rest of the afternoon in the lobby, going for only a short walk in the better part of town, and then had supper in the hotel dining room. At nine, Ted saw her to her room and said good night. The tension that had come up between them had not abated.

A few hours earlier two men sat at a table in the back of the Silver Saddle Saloon. One was Marty Fitzpatrick, looking just as unkempt as he had when on the trail. He was unshaven, and his shirt was soiled with sweat stains under the arms and down the back. Sitting with him was Butch Kraft, a skinny eighteen-year-old kid with a pimply face who was seriously lacking in self-esteem. He had arrived several days back on a cattle drive from Texas.

"What you were saying to everyone sure made sense to me, Mr. Fitzpatrick. These saloon people shot down one of us in cold blood. And it wasn't the first time. We should have ridden in here and burned down the whole town just like you said, including this bar we're at right now."

Marty gave a derisive laugh. "I thought we were about ready to ride on the town, and then old Joe Thompson, the manager of the holding pens, talked them out of it. Him and a few of the other cowboys, including my ex-trail boss, Buck McNurty. I surly do hate that man."

"I can't believe they blame all that shooting on old Hugh Anderson. I guess the Marshal ain't any too anxious to serve that warrant on him. He'd have to answer to a pretty big group of us cowhands if he tried."

"When the good Marshal tries to serve that warrant, all hell is going to break loose. You can take my word on that. We should have strung up that coroner's jury just like we threatened. Guess we scared some of them out of town, though." Marty took a sip of whiskey and thought a minute, his brow wrinkled with the effort. "The foreman, the gent that runs the bakery, is still around. Saw him in the hotel with that girlfriend of his. Been there all afternoon. You know, Butch, we could still stir up some excitement. Maybe trigger things to heat up." Marty was not a man to stand up for a cause unless that cause would lead to his own profit. In the back of his mind, he related the burning of the town to essentially looting the town, and he hated to give up on the idea so easily.

"What if you and me killed that foreman?" he said. "The cowhands will get the blame. We've already threatened the jury if they didn't vamoose. The town people will have to retaliate, and we might get things back on track after all."

"Golly, Mr. Fitzpatrick. You sure got a head on those shoulders of yours. I'm all for it."

"Then finish your drink, and let's get on with it."

Marty and Butch left the Silver Saddle Saloon and headed north on the dusty, moon-lit street. They crossed the railroad tracks and walked up to the Kansas Hotel. There was little activity in this part of town. The businesses were all closed and dark. The only light came from the hotel itself. Marty sauntered up to one of the windows and looked inside. Ted and Linda were sitting in the lobby in casual conversation. Other than the clerk at the desk, nobody else was visible. Ted was talking to his girl, and something he said made her laugh. Marty boiled over with jealously and resentment. The thought of two people happy with each other and oblivious to the world made him furious. *We'll soon change that*, he thought.

"C'mon, Butch. We'll wait down the street in that alley we just passed. It's late, and he'll be coming out pretty soon I would wager." The two men moved down the road and disappeared into the night.

After saying good night to Linda, Ted left the hotel and entered the dark street. On the other end of town, he could hear piano music coming from the saloons, loud laughter, and occasional shouting. In this part of the community, though, everything was quiet, and nobody stirred.

There was a three-quarter moon that alternated from shining brightly in the night sky and being obscured by passing clouds. As Ted walked up the road to his rooming house, he found himself searching the shadows for hidden danger. *Guess all that talk about a necktie party has got me more worked up than I care to admit.* A black-and-white cat sauntered from an alley, stopped when he saw Ted, and stared at him as if trying to cast a spell. Up the street a dog started barking, and Ted's uneasiness increased.

Suddenly two men appeared from a side street with bandanas over their faces and with guns drawn. Ted dove to the ground as they started shooting. A bullet plowed into the dirt by his face, and a second smashed into his leg. He was aware of another shot being fired from behind and he saw one of the two men drop his pistol, grab behind his chest that was starting to turn a crimson red, and topple over backward. The other man fired another wild shot, turned, and ran away.

"Senor Ted, are you hit bad?" It was Pedro, running up from behind with his pistol still in hand. He knelt beside Ted and looked at his blood-soaked pants leg.

After a minute, Ted said, "Just a flesh wound, I think. Where in tarnation did you come from?"

"I hear the rumors about the necktie party and I promise Miss Jenny that I will protect you. I have been waiting all evening for you to start back." Pedro grinned from ear to ear. "These hombres have more gonads than I thought, coming in front of you instead of from your back."

"Guess they knew I don't carry a gun. Pedro, I sure do owe you one."

Pedro tore Ted's pants leg open and wrapped a bandana around the wound and helped him to his feet. A small crowd had materialized, some standing around Ted and Pedro, and others examining the fallen assailant.

"Looks like you was bushwhacked for sure," someone said. "The killing was purely justified."

With Pedro's help, Ted hobbled over to look at the body. He didn't recognize him. It was a young man, his face covered with pimples.

"He's just a boy," Ted said.

CHAPTER 13

The next morning Ted was at the hotel at eight and had breakfast in the dining room with Linda. Doc Kern had bandaged his leg the night before, and Ted hoped the wrapping didn't make his pants leg bulge too much. He walked with a noticeable limp but told Linda that he had sprained his ankle. He didn't want her to know that he had been shot, or she would be in a complete frenzy. He had felt pretty good earlier but was beginning to experience some lethargy now. He hoped Linda didn't notice.

"Ted, I heard one of the maids saying that there had been another shooting last night. I swear this place is not safe to live in. Why don't you just get on the train and come home?"

"Linda, I am home. This is where I live. This is where we will live—you and I. Give the town a chance to mature, and it will be a wonderful place to live. We can have a great future here."

Linda sighed and made no further attempt to argue the point.

She left on the ten o'clock train. Ted had hoped that they might set the date for their wedding while she was there, but somehow the time never seemed right for discussing it.

After the train pulled out, Ted hobbled over to the post office to see Jenny. He was beginning to lose all of his energy and was feeling somewhat exhausted. As soon as she saw him, she stopped everything and came over to take his arm.

"Pedro told me about last night." She guided him to a chair. "Are you all right?"

"I'm fine. Just a flesh wound. Pedro said you were the one that had him looking out for me. I guess I owe you a big round of thanks for that."

"Think nothing of it. I was just worried that we might not have sour dough bread this week if anything happened to you."

Ted laughed. "Anyway, I do thank you."

"Did Linda get off okay?"

"Yep. She's on her way back to St. Louis. I don't think she was too impressed with our little town." Ted's voice was weak, and he felt tired.

"She'll come around. It just takes some getting used to. Any word yet on the other shooter? Pedro told me there were two of them."

"No, not that I've heard. The one that Pedro shot was just a boy, way too young to be mixed up with something like this."

"Like that kid that did all that shooting at Tuttle's. Riley, I think his name was? Nothing new on him either?"

"No. He just seems to have disappeared. I would bet he caught a train to parts unknown. And the Marshal hasn't arrested Anderson yet."

Jenny glanced down at Ted's pants leg and noticed it was stained with fresh blood. "Ted, you're bleeding! You should be in bed." Then she saw that he was perspiring slightly. "And you've got a fever! You sit right here. I'm going to get Doc Kern."

She rushed from the building and within minutes was back with the doctor in tow. He took one look at Ted, who was now flushed and feeling weak and trembling. "We've got to get this boy off his feet and in bed where I can examine him. I'm afraid infection has set in."

"Bring him back here," Jenny said without hesitation, indicating the room in the back of the post office. "Put him in my bed. I will move back into my room at Molly's now that Linda has gone."

"Jenny, I can't do that," Ted said. "I can't put you out."

"Well you're certainly not going to your room at the men's boarding house. Who'll take care of you there, with no women allowed? Get in there and get your clothes off so Doc can look you over."

With the doctor's help, Ted made it back to the bed and collapsed. His face was burning up, and soon he was beginning to slip in and out of consciousness.

———

A meeting of the merchants and leaders of the city was called by Judge Muse, and they were crowded together in the lobby of the Kansas Hotel.

"Quiet, everybody. Quiet. This meeting will now begin," the judge announced, standing on a chair to be better seen. "I want to thank everybody for coming. The events of the past few days, including last night, have made it abundantly clear that we are on the verge of becoming a lawless and violent community. Something must be done—and done immediately. If there is any doubt among you, let me read what is being said about last Saturday's shootings in the newspapers delivered on this morning's mail train."

The judge unfolded a copy of the *Emporia News* he had tucked under his arm and began to read:

"'It must be borne in mind that the state of society in that town'—meaning us—'is now at its worst. The town is largely inhabited by prostitutes, gamblers, and whiskey-sellers. Pistol shooting is the common amusement. All the frequenters of the saloons, gambling dens, and houses of ill-fame are armed at all times, mostly with two pistols.'

"And if you need further convincing, the *Topeka Daily Commonwealth* describes our fair city in even more colorful words." The judge produced another newspaper and recited, "'The air of Newton is tainted with the hot steam of human blood. Murder "most foul and unnatural" has again stained the pages of her short history, and the brand of Cain has stamped its crimson characters on the foreheads of men with horrible frequency.'"

The judge folded the paper and once again addressed the men assembled. "I think it is safe to say that none among us is desirous of such a reputation. So what must we do to redeem our good name? We are at this point still an unincorporated city. That means we have no tax authority, no city officials, and most importantly no police. Some of us have formed an informal committee, we are working on becoming incorporated, and the proper papers are being drawn up. But that is weeks and probably months away. In the meantime, we have to provide for our own security."

There was a murmur of agreement from the crowd.

"I think that is something that every segment of our town can agree on," the judge continued. "Joe Thompson, standing to my right and representing the cowboy contingent of our society, is as adamant as any for a peaceful community. He has assured me that the attack on Ted Baker last night was not a planned or condoned attack by the Texans. Mr. Baker, in fact, is highly regarded by all elements of our city. And the saloon owners, including Mr. Tuttle standing on my left, are equally desirous of bringing an end to violence. All of you merchants want to live in a community free from fear. None of us wants to have our establishments shot up or burned down. The problems we have been encountering are due to a small minority of our population. Some are laborers from the railroad, some are gamblers and whiskey peddlers, some are Texans up from cattle drives, but all of them are nothing more than riffraff that need to be dealt with. It is time for us to unite and proclaim that enough is enough!"

A round of applause went up from the audience. "What do you have in mind, Judge?" someone asked.

"It seems to me that we have two alternatives," the judge continued. "One is to admit we can't control the violence occurring in our city and to call in the army. I imagine a telegraph to the commanding general at Fort Harker would bring soldiers to our streets and martial law to our city within a matter of days. The other is for us to deal with the situation ourselves. We can all chip in and hire temporary deputies to police our community until we become incorporated and can hire permanent policemen. I personally prefer the latter, but it is up to the town to decide."

"It would take some pretty tough deputies to quiet this town," declared Thomas Lane, the owner of the Kansas Hotel. "Do you have anyone in mind?"

"There are some I could think of, but to do this right I think we should elect a committee to review possible applicants and make a selection."

"How about you, Judge? Will you serve on the committee?"

"I think it best if the committee comes from all of you. I don't want to be asserting myself into everything going on. Right now I have my hands full with the railroad land office, my construction business, and drawing up papers for incorporation."

"Sounds like the right approach to me," Zeb Turner said. "I move that we accept the judge's recommendation and get on with it. Anyone disagree?"

The crowd voiced their approval and proceeded to select a committee of five to hire two deputies for the city. One of the committee members was Wally Tomney, even though he was currently in Florence.

"He'll be on the next train back now that he knows we are moving to enforce the peace," Tony Albright said. "Nobody holds the welfare of our town in higher regard than him."

As soon as Buck and Katrina heard that Ted had been shot, they rushed over to the post office.

"How is he?" Buck asked Jenny.

"He's running a fever and is delirious most of the time. But the doctor thinks he will be okay."

"I think he is strong man," Katrina said. "He will make the recovery."

"I sure hope so," Jenny said.

"I do not understand this violence," Katrina said. "Every man seems to think the only way to settle the argument is to pull the gun and shoot at each other. It is crazy, I believe."

"They say the one that was killed is only a boy," Jenny said. "Do we have any idea who the other one was that got away?"

"Nobody got a look at him," Buck said. "But I bet I could make a pretty good guess. If it's who I suspect, he is nothing but a mean, cowardly cowpoke that ought to be horse-whipped and hung from the rafters." As soon as he said these words, Buck stole a quick look at Katrina, who had a slight frown on her face. He hastily added, "What I mean is, he ought to be brought to justice. By the way, who is staying with Ted at night?"

"I've brought a cot in beside the bed. Pedro says he will spend the night. Only trouble is that he needs to get up at four in the morning to bake bread and pastries and open the shop."

"No need for him to do that," Buck said. "I can spend the night here. I'm at an impasse waiting for lumber for the house and barn I'm building on my new farm. Might as well sleep here."

"And Mr. Pedro, I am thinking, must some help need," Katrina said. "He cannot bake the bread and sell at the counter at the same time. I will help him."

"Oh, Katrina, that would mean so much to Ted, I'm sure. Would you know what to do?"

"Is no problem. Is three cents for the donuts, five cents for the pastries, and eight cents for the bread. This I can do."

"So have your parents found land yet that they like?" Jenny asked.

"Yes, to the north and west. They have bought the land, and they write to everyone in our village that they must come to Kansas. And bring the Turkey Red wheat seeds for the planting. Someday all this land will grow the grain instead of the grass. It will be the big breadbasket."

CHAPTER 14

Rupert Anderson was a genial man, his white hair and expanding waist testifying to the fact that he was no longer the energetic, hard-working cowman that he had once been. He had two sons, Hugh and Richmond, both of whom had disappointed him by their brash and wayward episodes. Now Hugh, severely wounded, was wanted for murder. The only reason the sheriff hadn't arrested him yet was because he was being guarded by a dozen Texans, but it would only be a matter of time.

The aging Anderson sought out Judge Muse and R. M. Spivey. "You gentlemen know, I'm sure, the distress that your children can cause you. Hugh is a good boy. Anybody who knows him will vouch for that."

"He may be a good boy," the judge said, "but he sure enough killed a man in cold blood."

"No. Not in cold blood. McCluskie had his gun out and was waiting for him. It was only in the cards that were dealt to them that Hugh was wounded while McCluskie died. You boys know that out here these confrontations occur all the time."

"We are all too well aware of that, Mr. Anderson," the judge replied. "And if we are going to have a decent community for our children to grow up in, they have to stop. Responsible citizens cannot condone people killing each other over some dispute."

"Not just a dispute, Judge. It was to bring about justice. McCluskie had blatantly killed Hugh's friend, and the law wouldn't do anything about it. Surely you gentlemen understand honor and fairness. What if it had been your friend or brother or somebody close to you and nobody could touch the killer? And him sitting in a saloon, boasting and smoking cigars and playing cards like he was King of the Spread. Can you blame my son for wanting to right a terrible wrong?"

The judge and Spivey looked at each other, both of them sympathetic to what Anderson was saying.

"We understand your feelings, Anderson," Spivey said. "But the fact remains that five men were killed and three more wounded because your son decided to take the law into his own hands. It will be a long time before this town can live down the reputation it has gotten as a lawless and brutal community."

"That's just the point, gentlemen. What has happened already will be nothing compared to what will happen when the sheriff tries to arrest Hugh. There are a dozen Texans ready to shoot up and burn down this town when that happens. I beg you for my son's sake and for the safety of your community to help me get Hugh away. Likely he will die anyway, but let it be by God's will rather than ours. And let this be the end of this tragedy rather than the beginning of an even greater one."

The judge and Spivey sat for a long time, deliberating over Anderson's plea. Finally Spivey admitted, "I guess he's got a point, Judge. We sure don't need to spill any more blood to try to rectify what's already been done. And if we can spare this town any more bloodshed, shouldn't we do it?"

Judge Muse nodded in agreement. "If he is to be smuggled out of our fair community, it will have to be by train. With his wounds, I doubt that he could survive a rough wagon trip, and it would be easy for the sheriff to catch up with it. No, it's got to be by train."

"Trouble is, the sheriff has been walking through the trains before they pull out to make sure that doesn't happen. This is going to be a little tricky."

Two days later, at two in the morning, the back door of the El Dorado Hotel and Saloon opened, and three men crept out, pausing to make sure the way was clear before proceeding cautiously down the alley. The man in the middle had his arms around the shoulders of the other two and walked with considerable difficulty. They made their way north to the train tracks where the early morning express was sitting, ready to pull out for the east at four.

The night was cold and rainy, making progress difficult through the mixture of wet grass and mud. The good news was that nobody else was out and about in the nasty weather at this early hour.

"The conductor said it would be the fourth car back," the judge said. "The one next to the coal chutes."

The trio made their way to the passenger car in question. The door at the front was unlocked as promised, and the three men climbed into the car.

"Now, Hugh, we are going to put you in the toilet closet, and you lock the door from the inside. You stay there until the train is well on its way to Kansas City. Your father will be riding in the car, and you go sit beside him when you come out. You got all that?"

"I got it," Hugh Anderson replied. "But what if the sheriff checks the train?"

"He'll probably do that. But normally the cars are kept locked until time for the passengers to board, and the closets are kept locked until the train is well out of town. So he will expect your door to be locked and nobody inside."

"I can't thank you gentlemen enough for helping me."

"We're not doing this for you. We just don't want any more bloodshed, and that would surely be the case if the sheriff tried to arrest you. Your cowboy friends have made that pretty clear."

Hugh Anderson locked himself in the closet, and the other two left.

At 4:00 a.m., the train pulled out for Emporia and Kansas City right on time. Hugh Anderson had made his escape.

CHAPTER 15

Tom Carson was a big man, almost six feet tall, and hard. His brown hair hung over his forehead and over a face that exuded strength and determination. His eyes, however, were small and squinty, which hinted at a possible streak of meanness. He moved with a dexterity that indicated a supple body beneath the long, gray suit jacket he wore. Underneath the coat but still visible was a gun belt with a Colt .44 in the holster, commonly referred to as "the peacemaker."

Beside him was Carlos King, the deputy sheriff for Sedgwick County. Carlos was well respected in the community.

"These are the two men our committee has hired as acting deputy sheriff and acting constable for our fine town," Wally Tomney said. "Tom Carson, on my right, is just the kind of man we need. As some of you might know, he is the nephew of our famous frontiersman, Kit Carson. He has ample experience in dealing with the type of situation we have here in Newton. Since last June, Tom has served as deputy sheriff to Marshal Bill Hickok up in Abilene, known to some of you as 'Wild Bill Hickok.'

He has faced down hardened desperados such as John Wesley Hardin. I don't believe we could have found a more qualified man for this position if we searched for a hundred years.

"Standing next to him is a man you all know. Carlos B. King. He has been around our fair city since we were established, mostly as a deputy sheriff for Sedgwick County. He has a distinguished record as a Union soldier in the late War Between the States, having served in two Michigan units. He is a beloved Newtonian and will make an excellent acting constable."

Carlos was not a big man. In fact, he stood shorter than most and had a thin, wiry body. His face was also lacking in any unusual features, except that he always had a ready grin and friendly greeting for anyone he met.

"We all know Carlos," George Lovett said. He was one of the partners in the new Lovett, Bentley, Muse Construction Company. "But Mr. Carson is not a local gent. I've heard that he was in some kind of trouble up in Abilene. Would you care to comment on that, Mr. Carson?"

"Not much of a problem," Tom Carson replied. "I just got into a little fracas with a fellow deputy who I thought was shirking some of his duties. It was not a big deal."

"But isn't it true that you received an official reprimand?"

"Yes, I did." Carson's eyes hardened, and his voice took on a more belligerent tone. "And that's the main reason I left Abilene. When I wear a badge for a town, I expect the town to support me. If you're not willing to do that, say so right now. I'm not risking my life for a bunch of people who are going to turn on me at the first excuse."

The answer didn't satisfy Lovett, but he said nothing more.

"So as your first official act will you be arresting Hugh Anderson?" Tony Albright asked.

Carson gave Tomney a questioning look. "Do you care to answer that, Mr. Tomney?" Tomney looked a little uncomfortable as he stammered for words. "Matter of fact," he finally said, "it would appear that Mr. Anderson is not here."

"What?" roared a voice from the back of the room.

"I'm afraid that Mr. Anderson was not as badly wounded as we were led to believe, and he has in fact flown the coop."

"Are you telling me that you let that no-good murdering skunk get away?" The speaker was a large man with shaggy, uncombed black hair, a full black beard, and bulging eyes. "That man murdered my brother in cold blood, and he just walks away?"

Arthur McCluskie had come to Newton to bury his brother and to make sure that justice was served. He threw a chair against the wall and yelled a string of oaths to no one in particular. "I'll find that son of Satan if it takes forever. I'll cut his gizzard out while he's still alive and make him eat it. If the law can't handle this, then I will." He stormed from the hotel, leaving a shocked and silent crowd behind him.

"So Tomney," Thomas Lane returned to the subject at hand, "how much money did your committee raise? Enough to hire these two deputies for several months?"

"Yes. Everyone was most generous. I don't recall the exact amount right off, but I would say at fifty dollars a month each, we have enough for three or four months of these gents services. Maybe by then we will be incorporated and can hire a permanent police force."

"You were asking about my first official act," Tom Carson said. "Well, here it is. As of this moment, nobody is allowed to wear firearms while in the city. The committee here supports me in this. Anyone caught with a gun will have it confiscated."

A murmur of approval ran through the crowd.

"Sounds like we're finally going to get some law and order in this here place," someone said.

For the next several weeks the town remained calm with no further violence. The Texans knew Tom Carson as someone who was hard on cowboys, and some threatened to kill him on sight, but nothing came of it. The dog days of August slowly gave way to September. Ted Baker was recovering and getting restless at being laid up.

"Jenny, I am absolutely getting out of here tomorrow morning. I know better than the doc at this stage of the game just how I feel and what I can do."

"Ted Baker, you are a poor patient. What am I to do with you?"

"Well, you can spare me from having to read anymore of your dime novel magazines." He picked up the latest issue of *The Fireside Companion* and read from the table of contents. "*Little Goldie: A Story of a Woman's Love.* Now that's what I call fascinating reading. Although I will admit the *Old Sleuth* story was a little more interesting. A young detective whose favorite disguise is to dress up as an old man while he's snooping around. Maybe that's what Marshall Kennedy should have done to have gotten into the El Dorado to arrest Anderson."

Carlos King came into the post office and went directly to the back room. "How's our star patient doing?" he asked Jenny.

"He's being difficult," she replied.

"Hi, Carlos," Ted said. "Arrested any drunks yet today?"

"Nope. Things have been pretty quiet and orderly since we posted the 'no guns' posters. Most everybody seems to be abiding by the statute. Haven't gotten any leads on the hombre that shot you. And no sign of the Riley kid, nor of Anderson. I 'spect we'll not see hide nor hair of either one of them. Anderson's pa is a rich rancher down in Texas. Likely he'll head down that way. Nobody will touch him down there."

"I hear McCluskie's brother is pretty upset about Anderson getting away."

"He is for a fact. He's been roaring around town saying what he'll do if he ever sees him again. I reckon he'll cool down in time. By the way, I think you need to talk with Pedro over at your shop."

"Pedro? What's he done to get in trouble with the law?"

"It's not what he's done. It's what he isn't doing. When you ran the shop, as I recall, you used to give us upholders of the peace a free donut for risking our lives to protect the community. Pedro seems to think we should pay just like everyone else. He's a hard man, that one is."

Ted laughed. "Well, I won't have to have words with him. I plan to be back on the job myself tomorrow. You are welcome to a free donut anytime. But I expect you to pay for the coffee."

That evening Tom Carson and Carlos King made their usual rounds at the twenty-five saloon and gambling houses in Hyde Park. Honky-tonk piano music, loud laughter, and shouts spilled from every establishment onto the dirt street where cowboys, railroad workers, and others looking for a good time moved about.

At the Blum Saloon, Tom Carson ran across a cowboy who was drunk, barely able to walk, and who was threatening to burn down the whole town. Carson escorted this gent to the building that had been hastily converted to a jailhouse and locked him in a back room to sleep it off.

Carlos meandered on down the street, checking each establishment At the Dew Drop Inn, he spotted a cowboy at the bar who had a pistol strapped to his side. He had a few drinks under his belt and was talking in a loud voice. Carlos walked over to him. "Even', mister," he said. "You enjoying yourself?"

The cowboy turned and stared at Carlos. 'That I am, pardner. Been on the range for three months with nothing to drink but brackish water. This here whiskey tastes mighty good." He was in his twenties, about the same size as Carlos, and had a weathered face and week-old stubble of beard.

"My name's Carlos King," Carlos said. "I'm the acting constable for Newton."

"And mine's Tom Edwards, if anybody wants to know."

"Tom, we have a new ordinance in Newton," Carlos said. "Firearms are forbidden. I'm afraid I'm going to have to ask you for yours."

'You mean this one?" He pulled his gun from the holster and held it loosely in his hand. "Well now, me and this firearm have gotten to be pretty good friends. I don't cotton to the thought of parting company with it just because some con-sta-ble," he drew the word out, "gets himself all nervous over it. I do believe I'll just hold on to it."

"Tom, there's no need to make an issue over this. Just hand me your gun and you can get it back at our temporary office up the street when you're ready to leave town. In the meantime, you can enjoy yourself all you want with my blessing."

"I don't think you understand the situation here, Deputy. You see, I've got my gun in my hand and kinda pointing your way, and yours is in your holster. I don't plan to give it up, and if you go for your firearm, I'll just have to shoot you in self-defense. Now I would suggest that you just go on your way and leave me to my drinking. Which way do you want it?"

The crowd in the saloon, which had been watching the encounter, moved back and out of the line of fire of either man. The woman playing the piano stopped and left the bench. A silence fell over the establishment.

Carlos stared at the cowboy, debating his chances. He was just about to throw a punch at the man when he saw the butt of a rifle crash into the man's skull from behind. The cowboy's eyes rolled back in his head, he dropped the pistol, and slumped to the floor.

"You gave him too much of an advantage," Tom Carson said, lowering his rifle. "When you confront a man, you need to make sure you got the drop on him. Never give him an even break."

"Guess I owe you one," Carlos said. "He seemed harmless enough." Carlos bent over, picked up the man's gun, and stuck it in his waist.

The cowboy moaned and slowly sat up, holding the back of his head. Carlos picked up the man's drink from the bar and handed it to him. "Drink this. It'll make you feel better."

Edwards downed the whiskey and struggled to his feet.

Tom Carson grabbed him by the front of his shirt and pulled him close. "You're lucky I didn't kill you, cowboy. Pulling a pistol on a deputy is a killin' offense in my book. Now you get yourself out of this town and don't come back, or next time you'll be staying permanently." He gave the man a shove. He fell back against the bar and then staggered from the saloon.

"That was a little harsh, Tom," Carlos said. "I don't think the man was really that dangerous. Just had a little too much to drink."

Carson gave Carlos a look of disgust. "These hombres can be mean, Carlos. The only way to handle them is to be even meaner. You don't want them to like you. You want them to be scared of you."

The crowd moved back to the bar, and the saloon returned to life. The woman at the piano began playing and singing a rendition of "The Wildwood Flower":

> "I'll sing and I'll dance and my laugh shall be gay.
> I'll charm every heart and the crowd I will sway.
> I'll live you to see him regret the dark hour
> When he won and neglected this frail wildwood flower."

"Carlos, things are pretty quiet tonight," Carson said. "I don't think there will be any further trouble. I've got me a little business to attend to up the street, if you know what I mean." He gave an exaggerated wink and ambled off.

Carlos suspected the "business" that needed tending was a redheaded saloon girl that had been making eyes at Carson the past few days.

Carlos mingled with the people at the bar, refusing the drinks that were offered him. Most were friendly enough, but a few of the cowboys gave him sullen looks. They weren't happy about the way Carson had treated one of their own.

At midnight, Carlos was standing just outside of Rowdy Joe's Dance Hall where the evening's festivities were in full swing. Two cowboys staggered out of the door and into the street, arms around each other, and singing a slurred version of "Old Lang Syne." One of them spotted Carlos and gave him a half-hearted salute.

"Howdy, Constable," he said.

Carlos smiled. "Good evening, Josh. Hope you are enjoying yourself on this fine night."

"Yes, sir, we're having a grand old time. Ain't we, Johnnie?" The other cowboy nodded in agreement, mumbled something unintelligible, and they moved unsteadily on down the street.

Carlos stopped to light a cigarette and watched as another wrangler led his horse up the dirt road. As he drew nearer, he recognized Tom Edwards, the cowpoke they had disarmed several hours earlier. Carlos spoke to him as he drew near.

"Edwards, as I recall, Marshal Carson ordered you out of town. Now I know the Marshal pretty well, and I don't think I'd be going against his word."

"Yes, sir. Yes, sir. I surely do heed the Marshal's advice. I've got my bedroll all wrapped up on my horse, and I'm just about ready to head south. Good night for traveling, don't you think?"

"Good as any, I reckon."

"I just got me one thing left to do before I light out. Is the Marshal around?"

"No, he's not. Anything I can do for you?"

"Guess you'll have to be the one then." Edwards pulled a derringer from his pocket, placed it against the chest of Carlos, and fired. Carlos staggered back, a shocked look on his face, and then fell to his knees.

Edwards leaped on his horse, gave a wild rebel yell, and rode off into the darkness.

Several cowboys rushed from the saloon and knelt to help Carlos, but he was fading fast.

"Did that man shoot me?" he asked in a feeble voice; then his eyes rolled up into his head, and he died.

All of the stores in Newton closed the next afternoon for the funeral of Carlos King. He was the first person to be buried in Newton's new Greenwood Cemetery, and the first peace officer to be killed in the line of duty for Sedgwick County. The *Kansas Daily Commonwealth* of Topeka paid this tribute to him: "Thus perished Officer King, whom there was no better gentleman and truer friend, and no more respected man in Newton."

CHAPTER 16

For the rest of September and October, things remained quiet in Newton. Then on October 30, the weather turned cold. It started with a twenty-degree dip in the temperature in one hour and kept going down. The wind came up, blinding everyone with swirling dust; then the dust turned to freezing rain and snow. Businesses closed for the day although it was only two in the afternoon.

At Ted's Bakery, the fires blazed brightly in the cooking ovens, trying to dispel the cold blasts of air that seeped in through the walls. The front door slammed open, and Pedro came in, struggling to close the door behind him.

"Holy Mother, I have never seen such a wind," Pedro said. "I think the temperature, she is at ten. I do not believe we will have the customers today. The streets they are empty. Not even a horse did I see."

"It's pretty miserable all right," Ted said. "How is Jenny doing?"

Pedro had gone to the post office to check for mail, but Ted thought that secretly he wanted to make sure the postmistress was okay. Which was exactly the same concern that Ted had.

"She is fine. She has the blankets wrapped around her to keep warm. I think it will be a long night. She had this one letter from Miss Linda for you." He dug into his coat pocket and produced a somewhat crumpled letter.

Ted took the envelope from him, not sure that he liked having it public knowledge every time he got a letter from his fiancé. He opened it and began to read. Pedro waited expectantly, curious to know what news she might have. Finally he said, "Everything is okay? Miss Linda is fine?"

"Good grief. Can't a man have any secrets around here? Yes, she is great. Says she is sorry for the way she acted when she was here and now realizes that she is not going to be able to talk me into leaving Newton. She is ready to get married and move into our new home here."

"*Buena*! Is good, no?"

"No. I mean, yes. I am a very lucky man, Pedro."

"*Si*. I think so."

The door swung open, and Buck McNurty came in, brushing snow from his jacket.

"I thought you might be open," he said. "Probably the only place in our little city except for a couple of the saloons."

"Hi, Buck. How come you're out in weather like this?"

"Got stuck. I came to town for some supplies, and this dad-blamed storm came up before I even knew it was coming. You can't even see across the street out there. I took my horses and wagon down to the livery. Old Jake was still around, so I was able to get them into some protection in the barn. I fear for all the cattle out in the holding pens. This is a killer storm, and they'll be lucky to survive."

"Where are you spending the night, Buck?"

"Down at the stables with the horses. I got a bed roll down there."

"No need for that, Buck. The fireplace in my home isn't finished yet, so Pedro and I are planning on staying here till this blows over. Bring your bedroll up here and join us."

"Now that's the best offer I've had all day. You can bring me up to date on all the local news. I've been so busy at my farm that I hardly get to town anymore."

The three men sat down in front of the oven, warming their hands over the glowing coals.

"Guess you heard about Tomney and his fellow Republicans getting short changed down in Wichita at the nominating convention?"

"Something about it. Wichita cut down the number of delegates we were allowed?'

"Yep. We sent seven representatives based on our estimate of Newton's current population, but the other delegates from the county said this figure was greatly overblown—that we shouldn't be able to count all the Texans that came up on cattle drives, as they weren't permanent residents. So they cut our seven down to three. Got old Tomney all riled up. Even Judge Muse got pretty mad. Our delegation ended up walking out and came up with their own list of candidates. Bottom line is that we are for sure now pushing to break away from Sedgwick. Promised Governor Harvey that we would name the new county after him if he pushes it through."

"Harvey County. Has a good ring to it."

"This Governor Harvey. He is a good man?" Pedro asked.

"One of the best. Has the nickname of 'Old Honesty.' He formed a regiment during the Civil War and served as a captain. He wasn't going to run for governor because he didn't have the money for a campaign, but a friend loaned him two hundred dollars, so he decided to do it. Been a fine governor and well liked."

"Any word on the hombre that killed Carlos?" Buck asked.

"Nobody has seen hide or hair of him. Seems he lit out right after he shot King and never looked back. I doubt we will ever hear from him, or from the kid Jim Riley, or Hugh Anderson. All of our killers seem to walk away free as jailbirds. And I hear that Sheriff Carson is thinking about returning to Abilene. I think he's been spooked every since King was shot."

"It would be good riddance as far as I am concerned," Buck said. "That man is pure poison. I don't know which is worse—him or the ruffians and cutthroats hanging out in the saloons."

"By the way, how are things with Katrina?"

"Good. Her folks bought land a few miles north and west of here. Started building their house and barn. It's good land. Katy says they are writing to everyone in their village to come to Kansas."

"Have you set a date for the wedding?"

"Next spring. Right after I get the corn planted. Thought we would go to Kansas City for a few days for our honeymoon. How about you and Linda?"

"Haven't decided on a definite date as yet. I think she is reconciled to living in Newton, though. That's a step in the right direction. I take it you've given up all hope of ever finding the two men who killed your parents?"

"I reckon I'll have to leave that in God's hands. Probably just as good. If I ever found them, I'd have to kill them, and that sure wouldn't set very well with Katy."

Ted threw more wood onto the fire burning in the ovens. Outside the wind hammered against the front of the building, and the snow piled high in front of the door.

CHAPTER 17

There were no reported human deaths from the Blizzard of 1871, but the cattle in the area were not so fortunate. In the holding pens there was no protection from the biting sleet and snow. The cows huddled together in a vain effort to fight off the wind, but one by one they began to fall. Those still out on the prairie fared a little better when they could find a ravine or bushes to give them some protection. But hundreds of cattle died in the storm. For weeks afterwards the wintery air around Newton was filled with the smoke of burning carcasses.

The tension that had built up over the Hyde Park Massacre, as it was being called, gradually eased. There were reports that Hugh Anderson had returned to his father's ranch in Texas and would recover from his wounds. Arthur McCluskie remained in town, vowing that someday the time would come when he would get even with Anderson for killing his brother. Nothing was ever heard from Jim Riley. Everyone assumed that he had found some place quiet to end his days.

Tom Carson remained as the city marshal until the end of November, when he resigned and returned to

Abilene. Newton's third sheriff was William Brooks, more commonly known as "Bully" Brooks because of his aggressive nature. Work was well along on laying track to Wichita, and some of the rough crowd was beginning to move south in anticipation of Wichita being the next end of the trail for cattle drives coming up from Texas. But 1872 would still see the herds coming to Newton for most of the year, and the city remained the rowdy and violent town that had marked its first year when thirty to forty thousand cattle had made their way north.

The Kansas Legislature approved Newton breaking off from Sedgwick County in February of 1872. The new county took three townships from McPherson County, three from Marion County, and ten from Sedgwick. At the same time, the governor approved the incorporation of Newton as a city of the third class and named it as the temporary county seat.

The spring of 1872 was beautiful in Kansas. The fields were a carpet of multicolored flowers: purple violets, red and pink morning glories, and cushions of white elderberries. It was a time of new birth, not only for plants and trees but also for the hopes and aspirations of those who had endured a long and harsh winter. This enthusiasm was nowhere more apparent than in Ted's Bakery.

"I trust I can count on everyone's support." Wally Tomney spoke to six citizens sitting around tables, sipping hot coffee and munching donuts. "It is a crucial time in our county, and we need strong leadership and someone committed to law and order." Wally Tomney was running for county supervisor of the new county.

"Speaking of law and order," Ted said from behind the counter, "I don't believe we ever did get an accounting of all the money we raised to hire Carson and King. How much did we bring in, and how much did we spend?"

Tomney gave Ted a hard look. "I don't believe a strict accounting is necessary. I didn't keep records on who gave what, but by the time we paid the deputies salary, rent for a temporary office and jail, printing and other expenses, there wasn't anything left. These were all donations and handled on an informal basis."

"Seems to me anytime you are handling someone else's funds there should be a detailed record kept," Ted replied.

Tomney glowered at Ted but didn't reply. As he headed for the door, he turned and addressed the others in the shop. "Remember, folks, be sure to vote. And even if you don't vote for me, at least vote." With that, he waved at the group and left.

Governor Harvey had appointed a temporary slate of officers for Harvey County and the city of Newton when the county was created, but now the citizens of these new entities were holding their first general election to select their own officers. The governor's appointees except for one were all on the ballot, mostly unopposed. But Wally Tomney and a few of the others had candidates running against them.

"I think it is written somewhere that whenever two or more are gathered in my name, Tomney will be there to make a speech," Ted said.

"Trouble is," Tony Albright said, "I never even heard of most of the people on the slate. Who's this Adrian

Smith running for county treasurer? He just seemed to appear out of nowhere."

"Some friend or acquaintance of Tomney, I 'spect," Zeb Turner said. "I understand he's the one that came up with names for most of the offices."

"Well for my money, it's too bad Judge Muse isn't running for county supervisor," Martha King said. Ted had hired Carlos King's widow to work in his store, and she had been an added attraction for the morning coffee group. Carlos was still remembered as a popular and dedicated citizen of the new city.

"He would win hands down, that's for sure," George Lovett said. "But he says he's got his fingers into too many pies already. Says politics aren't his cup of tea."

"If you gents will excuse me," Ted said, "I need to go down the post office and see how many bills I owe. Martha, keep good care of these paying customers while I'm gone."

"As long as they're paying, they'll get good service," Martha replied.

———————

At the post office, Ted found a young man leaning on the counter across from Jenny, tapping on the surface with a gold coin. Jenny was in deep concentration but finally looked up and saw Ted.

"Come on in, Ted," she said. "Alan is teaching me Morse code." Turning back to the stranger, she said, "I think you said 'hello, Johnnie.'"

"Close, but not quite right. It was 'hello, Jenny.'"

Jenny laughed. "I guess I should have guessed that one. Ted, do you know Alan? Alan Asher. He is with the railroad. And this is Ted Baker, a good guy to know. He owns the bakery across the street."

"Don't think I've had the pleasure," Ted said with luke-warm enthusiasm.

Alan stepped forward and extended his hand. "Glad to meet you, Ted. I'm the new dispatcher for the Santa Fe Railroad. Now that we're almost to Wichita to the south and to Dodge to the west, the powers that be thought it was time to establish a dispatcher here in Newton."

Alan was about the same height as Ted but a little broader across the shoulders. He was good looking with sandy hair and deep-blue eyes. When he smiled, his whole face seemed to light up. He seemed a very personable individual, and Ted immediately took a dislike to him.

"How are the land sales going?" Ted asked. The AT&SF had received a land grant of three million acres from the government to promote settlement in the west.

"Doing just great," Alan replied. "The company is offering discounted fares to anyone who wants to come out here and inspect the terrain, and if they end up buying land, the railroad will apply the full price of the ticket toward the sale."

"Ought to be good for business," Ted said.

"Well, I'd better get back to my office," Alan said. "Can't keep the trains waiting, can we? Maybe I'll drop back this afternoon, Jenny, and we can practice some more on the Morse code. Never know when that knowledge can come in handy."

"Sounds good, Alan. I'll be looking for you."

After he left Ted said, without much conviction, "Seems like a nice person."

"Oh, he is," Jenny said. "I think he will be a good addition to our growing town. No letter for you today from Linda, I'm afraid. Have you two set a date yet for the wedding?"

"September 14. It's going to be back in St. Louis. Our house is finished here, and I'm moving into it on Monday. Afraid I'm not much on decorations, but Pedro knows a carpenter who is making a dining table and chairs and cabinet for us." After an awkward silence— awkward because he wanted to ask if Jenny was taking a shine to the new railroad man even though he knew it was none of his business—he said, "Tomney was just in the shop. I swear I can't abide that man."

"Well, we need a county supervisor, and he is working hard enough to get the job. Any idea who we will hire as our very first police chief?"

"Another case of nobody worthwhile wanting the job. I hear that it's going to be Bill Brooks, He's mean enough for the job, that's for sure, but he is also a bully and a hothead."

"Oh, Ted. You get too worked up over things. You need to relax and enjoy yourself more. Did you by any chance see the poem in the *Smith County Pioneer* that just came in this morning? Some homesteader up there wrote a poem about Kansas."

"Can't say I have."

"Then let me read it to you. It's called 'Home on the Range.'" She picked up a paper from the counter and began to read:

Oh give me a home,
Where the buffalo roam,
Where the deer and the antelope play,
Where seldom is heard,
A discouraging word,
And the sky is not cloudy all day.

How often at night, when the heavens were bright,
With the light of the twinkling stars
Have I stood here amazed, and asked as I gazed,
If their glory exceed that of ours.

I love the wild flowers in this bright land of ours,
I love the wild curlew's shrill scream;
The bluffs and white rocks, and antelope flocks
That graze on the mountains so green.

The air is so pure and the breezes so fine,
The zephyrs so balmy and light,
That I would not exchange my home here to range
Forever in azures so bright.

"Now, isn't that nice? The words are so positive. A land full of deer and antelope, and nobody complaining about anything. Makes you feel good."

"Must be a different Kansas up that a'way than down here," Ted replied with a smile. "But I like listening to you read. Almost sounds like it ought to be a song. Maybe someone will put it to music one of these days."

CHAPTER 18

By the summer of 1872, things in Newton were much calmer than they had been the previous year, with much of the cattle trade moving to Wichita. That community welcomed the rip-snorting, boisterous, and often violent crowd that accompanied the drives, posting a sign outside of town which declared in bold print: "Everything goes in Wichita."

But there were still a number of cowhands and gamblers frequenting the saloons and dance halls in Newton and a few cattle drives still bypassing Wichita. Newton's wild west days were not quite over, but already a new problem was surfacing in the town's infant political arena.

The first general election in the new county was held on May 20, 1872. Tomney and the officers that had been appointed by the governor were expected to be formally voted in to the offices they now held.

Ted Baker, Doc Kern, and Alan Asher manned one of the polling booths in the El Dorado Saloon.

"Jenny and I rode out in a wagon last week to see if we could spot any buffalo," Alan said. "I'd heard that there was a herd just to the north of town, but we couldn't find any. Had a nice ride, though, with a pretty girl," he added with a knowing smile.

What a blowhard, Ted thought. *Don't know what Jenny can see in him.* Alan was almost always in the post office these days whenever Ted was there.

"We've sure had a big turnout for the election," Ted said, wanting to change the subject.

"Yeah," Alan said. "Jenny and I figured that we'd have almost a one hundred percent vote. This is a big day for Newton. Jenny doesn't think we'll have any bigger turnout even for the presidential election this fall."

Why do I want to hit him in his big yapping mouth? Ted thought.

"Speaking of the presidential election," Doc Kern said, "who are you boys betting on—old Ulysses Grant or that upstart Horace Greely?"

Ulysses Grant was running for reelection on the Republican Party, and Greely was running on the new Liberal Republican Party ticket. The Democrats were unable to come up with a viable candidate so threw their support to the Liberal Republicans.

"The Liberals would sure be bad news for us," Alan said. "They want to discontinue granting land to the railroads to spur development. Wouldn't be no railroad here in Newton if we didn't have land to sell to homesteaders. There'd be no point in building a railroad to an unpopulated prairie."

In between their conversation, they were processing people waiting to vote by checking their names off on the official poll book. Ted asked the voters for their names and then watched as Alan checked them off on the poll book. Doc Kern gave them the ballot and, after it had been filled out, stuffed it in the ballot box.

As the day went on, it seemed to Ted that there was an unusually large number of voters coming through the line. A census had been taken on the first of April, and the poll books were presumably based on this survey, but it seemed like there were a lot of cowboys coming through the line who might not be permanent residents in Ted's view.

Around noon Ted noticed a rather large man in cowboy attire in the line waiting to vote that he was sure had been there earlier in the day. When the man got to the table, Ted said, "Hi there. Something I can help you with?"

"I'm here to vote," the man replied, a little unsteady on his feet. Ted could smell whiskey on his breath, although the saloons were all closed for the election.

"I think you've already voted, my friend. You were in earlier this morning."

"Nope. Haven't voted. Need to vote."

"I'm sure you're mistaken. I distinctly remember you. Around ten as I recall."

"Must have been somebody else that looked like me. Gimme a ballot." The man leaned in close, blowing alcohol fumes in Ted's face.

"What's your name?" Ted said. "We'll see if we have you checked off."

The man paused a minute, trying to think. "Peter," he finally said. "Peter Thom…somethin. Thompson. Or Tomkins. I get mixed up."

Alan checked the poll book. "No Peter Thompson here. Or Tomkins either."

"But I'm supposed to vote," the man said. "Gotta vote."

"I'm sorry, mister," Ted said. "You can't vote unless you're on the register. Please step aside and let the rest of these good people get processed."

The man stumbled back and out of the saloon, muttering to himself.

After this, Ted started examining the voters more closely and realized that many of them looked like voters who had been in earlier in the day.

"This is out and out fraud," he exclaimed to Doc Kern.

"But what can we do?" the doctor replied. "The names they give are on the poll book. We can't just turn them away because we think they voted under another name. Maybe the earlier vote was under a fraudulent name and this one is their legitimate name. How are we to know?"

"Someone has rigged the poll book, that's for sure," Ted replied, completely frustrated. He tried to think of a solution but reluctantly decided that the doc was right. "Guess we have to let them vote and complain afterward," he said.

———————

Four days later Ted appeared before the county commissioners who were canvassing the election returns.

"The voter registration list has been shamelessly altered to contain names of persons that are not citizens of Harvey County," he stated. "The names may not even be real people, just made-up names."

"Not made up," John Swanson, one of the commissioners, said. "Someone has recognized some of the names as being right out of the phone book of Cincinnati, Ohio. I guess those folk came all the way out here just to vote in our election."

"But what can we do about it?" Ted asked.

"Well, seems that two of the townships have recorded a far greater vote than the census figures would support," another of the commissioners said. "Newton township and Sedgwick. We know which names on those lists are fraudulent, but what we don't know is how they voted. I think we have no recourse but to throw out all of the votes for these two townships. No way to tell which votes were legitimate and which were phony. That leaves us with valid results from the other thirteen townships."

"What does that do for the election results?" Ted asked.

"Won't change anything. The same candidates win, with or without these ballots. And Newton is still voted as the county seat. Looks like someone went to a lot of trouble to rig an election that they won anyway."

"And I can guess who that someone might be," Ted said, thinking of their county supervisor, Wally Tomney. "But can't we figure out how those registers got altered?"

"The county clerk swears that the poll books were correct when they left his office. Somewhere or somehow the books got switched, but I reckon we'll never know the how of it."

Ted had the distinct impression that the county commissioners were not interested in pursuing the matter any further.

Chapter 19

August of 1872 was a busy month for Newton in spite of losing much of the cattle trade to Wichita. H. C. Ashbaugh, a new citizen of the town, started the first weekly newspaper, *The Newton Kansan*. Three thousand dollars in bonds were voted to build a brick schoolhouse, and Mary Boyd was hired as the schoolmistress. The First Presbyterian Church was organized but as yet had no full-time minister. Sunday school classes had been started the previous fall under the guidance of Judge Muse and were turned over to the churches as they became organized. And the city council passed an ordinance prohibiting the running at large of buffalo and other wild animals.

But the saloons and dance halls still flourished, and there were increasing reports of innocent people being swindled out of their money by con artists with very little being done by the law or county officials.

Later in the week Ted visited the offices of Wally Tomney, the county supervisor. The receptionist was a pretty girl in her twenties who Ted had never met before.

"Hi," he said, "I'm Ted Baker. I have an appointment to meet with Mr. Tomney."

"Oh, yes, Mr. Baker. Mr. Tomney will see you in a moment. Please have a seat."

Her speech was very slow and spoken in a high-pitched voice. The words sounded like a memorized recitation that had been carefully rehearsed, like a little girl reading from her first book. Ted smiled to himself. He could well imagine where the receptionist had worked before. Only then she probably wore a lot more rouge and lipstick.

Forty-five minutes later Ted was still waiting. No one had come or gone from the office.

"Would you please remind your boss that we had an eleven o'clock appointment, and it is now eleven forty-five," he said to the girl, who was applying fresh makeup for the third time since he had been there. "Just in case he forgot."

"Oh, he didn't forget, Mr. Baker," she replied. "He said you should just sit and wait a bit. He's very busy, you know."

"Well, I've waited. Now I'm going in."

He walked over and pulled the door to Tomney's office open over the feeble protests of the receptionist. Tomney was sitting at his desk studying some papers, smoking on a cigar hanging out of the corner of his mouth. He looked up as Ted stormed into the office.

"Oh, it's you," was all he said.

"Yes, it's me. Apparently you forgot about our appointment. Now, if you will just put those papers aside, we'll get on with our business."

"I'm not sure I like the tone in your voice, Ted. I must remind you that you are speaking to the supervisor of this county, an office that demands more respect than you are currently showing." He pulled a watch from his pocket, looked at it, and said, "It's almost lunchtime. However, I'll give you ten minutes, and then you're out of here."

"I'm well aware to whom I'm speaking," Ted said. "An elected official who is supposedly serving the people—and that's me, for one."

"All right, Ted. Simmer down. What's on your mind?"

Ted sat down and mentally counted to ten before speaking.

"Wally, we've got to do something to rein in the immoral and criminal actions of some of our saloons and gambling halls. I thought things would be better when many of them folded up and headed down to Wichita, but those that are left are worse than ever. They're holding some of their prostitutes in what amounts to slavery, and every day we hear of innocent people being swindled out of their money by the gamblers and con artists. I'm not sure it is even safe for a man to wander down to that part of town after dark."

"We enforce the laws, Ted. It is not our job to police the morals of the saloon workers or the people that choose to frequent their establishment."

"I wouldn't call slavery or robbery a mere moral question," Ted said. "Last time I looked, these were considered unlawful acts."

"And just what is it you would have us do?"

"I think the sheriff should question every prostitute working in the saloons and determine if they are being held against their will and to promise them sanctuary if they ever decide they want to leave but are afraid. I think the saloon owners should be put on notice that the town will not tolerate any shady dealings or shake downs of their customers. That any complaints will be vigorously prosecuted with the possibility of having their licenses revoked."

"Now you listen to me, young man." Tomney had turned almost purple listening to Ted's demands. "Those saloons are the lifeblood of this community. Any one of them pays more revenue to the city than all the rest of you merchants combined. If you and your so-called puritans drive these establishments out of business, it will be the ruin of Newton. I suggest that you start minding your own business for a change and leave the running of this county to those who know what they're doing. And if you need some help in doing that, there are those that would be more than happy to make sure you stop stirring up trouble. Do I make myself clear?"

"It couldn't be any clearer," Ted replied. "You are every bit as corrupt as I feared you'd be. Tomney, you are a disgrace to this county, and I'm going to fight you every chance I get."

Ted slammed his fist down on Tomney's desk so hard it made Tomney jump. For a minute, the two men glared at each other; then Ted turned and stormed out of the office.

CHAPTER 20

John "Gramps" Thompson was in a bed in the sick room of Doc Kern's office. Over the past two weeks, his health had deteriorated rapidly. He was unable to keep food down and had horrific pains in his stomach. The sweat rolled off his face as he labored for each breath. He didn't need the doctor to tell him that he was on his last legs.

When Doc Kern's wife, Nellie, came in to check on him, he motioned for her to come close. He raised himself up on one elbow and in a weak voice said, "I need to see Buck McNurty. Got something important to tell him. Get Buck for me." He fell back on the bed, closed his eyes, and labored with shallow breaths.

Nellie passed the request on to her husband, who thought for a moment. "Go find Charlie and tell him he needs to ride out to McNurty's farm and tell him that Thompson wants to see him. Says it is important. And tell him he'd better hurry because I don't think Thompson has much time left." Charlie was a youth who cleaned Doc's office twice a week.

Three hours later Buck and Katrina pulled up in a wagon in front of Doc's clinic. They dismounted, Buck tied the horses to the hitching post, and they came inside.

"He's in the back room," Doc said as soon as he saw them. Buck was in a pair of muddy overalls. He had obviously dropped everything and came to town without getting out of his work clothes. "He's in a bad way. Doubt that he'll last out the afternoon."

Buck and Katrina entered the room. Gramps was lying on his back with his eyes closed, struggling for each breath.

Buck went over to the bed, pulled up a chair, and took hold of Gramps's hand. "Hey, you old codger," he said in a soft voice. "What are you doing laying here pretending to be sick? You're scaring everyone half to death."

Gramps opened his eyes and turned his head to look at Buck. It took him a minute to focus on who was sitting there. Finally he said, "Got something to tell you, Buck. Should have done it a long time ago, but I didn't dare, or they'd have hung me for sure."

"Better be careful, old timer," Buck said with a chuckle. "Don't confess to somethin' you'll be sorry for when you get well."

"Ain't gonna get well, Buck. We both know that. What I got to tell you is…I was there when your ma and pa got killed."

Buck straightened in his chair. "What? What are you saying?"

"I met this feller in a bar in Sweetwater." Gramps struggled with his breathing, and his words came out slow and barely audible. Buck leaned in close, his whole body tense and a hard look replacing the soft features that had been there a second before.

"We were both headed west," Gramps continued, "so we decided to travel together. Sometimes a little safer thataway. I didn't really know anything about him, or him me, but he seemed like a friendly sort. As we was riding out of town, we came to your place. This feller says that a man who lives there owes him a ten spot and we should stop and collect. I thought it was kinda funny that he hadn't mentioned it before, but we rode up to the house. We got off our horses and went up to the door. When your pa opened it, this feller all of a sudden has his gun out and pushes your pa back into the room.

"Your pa was surprised and says, 'Who are you? What do you want here?' Your ma came up behind them. It dawned on me that this feller didn't know your dad after all and that he was getting ready to rob them. I started to protest, but he turned the gun on me and told me to shut up. It was then your pa grabbed for a rifle in the corner of the room, but this feller shot him three times. Then, while I stood there too dumbfounded to move, he shot your ma in cold blood."

Gramps stopped and turned his head away, coughing harshly. The spasm shook his whole body, and Buck could see blood dripping out of the corner of Gramps's mouth.

"Who was this man?" Buck said, a rising anger apparent in his voice. "What was his name?"

It was several minutes before Gramps could continue.

"I just stood there like an idiot, too surprised and revolted to think clearly. This feller turned his gun on me again and said, 'Either you're with me or against me. Which will it be? If you're against me, you die right here and now.' I guess I mumbled something in the affirmative. I don't rightly remember what I said, but this feller puts his gun away and says that if I ever say anything, he'll swear that this was all my idea. 'Likely we'll both hang,' he says, 'but I won't hang alone. So better learn to keep your trap shut.' He searched the house for any money while I stood there staring at your parents, wondering what I'd gotten myself into. When we rode out, we parted ways, him warning me again that if I ever said anything, I'd be strung up alongside him."

Buck grabbed Gramps by the shoulders, his face contorted with fury. "Who was it?" he demanded. "Who killed my ma and pa?"

Katrina put her hands on Buck's shoulder. "Buck, you must not be so angry. This is not good."

"Who was it?" Buck demanded again.

Gramps looked at Buck with watery, blood-filled eyes. "Please forgive me. I've wanted to tell you so many times since we've met. You've been good to me. After we parted company, I didn't see this feller again until we started the trail drive up here. It was Marty—Marty Fitzpatrick. That's why he was always picking on me. He wanted to kill me for sure but just couldn't find any good excuse."

Buck released his grip on Gramps's shoulder and sat there for a few minutes, his mind trying to absorb what he had just heard.

"Buck," Katrina said, "this man has asked for you to forgive him. You must do this. Do not build this hatred in your heart."

Buck's eyes, which had been focused on something far away, slowly returned to the room, and they softened once again as they looked at Gramps.

"I forgive you, old timer," he said. "Nothing really to forgive when it comes to that. I'd have done the same thing if I'd been in your boots. But Fitzpatrick will pay for what he did to my parents—and for what he did to you. His time has finally come. You rest easy, Gramps. We'll both get our satisfaction after these many years."

Katrina backed away from Buck, her hands to her mouth. "No, Buck. You must let it go. This is a matter for the sheriff. Let me get him now, and Gramps can tell him everything."

"Afraid not," Doc Kerns said. He had moved over to the bed and was looking down at Gramps. "I'm afraid Mr. Thompson has just left us." He pulled the sheet over Gramps's head.

Katrina moved to take Buck's arm. "But we all heard what he said. We can tell the sheriff everything."

"Wouldn't do any good," Buck said. "It's called 'hearsay' and not admissible in court. And anyway, who out here is interested in a shooting that took place in Illinois years ago? No. If justice is to be done, I'm the one that has to deliver it. Let's go home, Katrina. I need to change my clothes and to get some things."

"You mean to get your guns. This must not be, Buck. It is not your job to make the vengeance. God does not permit this. We will tell the sheriff."

"As I recall, the Bible says 'an eye for an eye.' That sounds like God recognizes that some things you got to do yourself."

"You have it wrong. Jesus says an 'eye for an eye' is not good, that if someone strikes you on the right cheek, you should turn the other. You must leave this to God to deal with this man."

"Marty Fitzpatrick has done more than strike my right cheek. He has killed my parents, and I have waited and searched for too many years to let him walk away from that. Are you coming or not?"

Katrina followed him out the door, still pleading for him to leave this in the hands of the law.

Doc Kerns watched them go and then hurried off to find Sheriff Brooks. He found him having lunch at the Dew Drop Inn.

"You'd better stop Buck, or there's going to be another killing. I don't give a fig about Fitzpatrick—he undoubtedly deserves being dismembered and fed to the hogs. But I'm worried about Buck. He's too good a man to get himself shot."

Brooks took another generous bite of steak while listening to Doc's story and then said between chews, "Seems to me Buck's got it right. No grounds to arrest Fitzpatrick. And no grounds to do anything about McNurty either."

"But can't you put him in jail for a few days till he cools down? After all, he has threatened to kill Fitzpatrick."

"Doc, if I arrested every man in this town who threatened to shoot somebody, there wouldn't be anyone left walking the streets. Not even you, I dare say."

William L. Brooks, Newton's third sheriff and first official city marshal, was a big man, well over six feet tall, with a thick neck, wide shoulders, and arms with bulging biceps. He had short black hair, a high forehead, and a face marked by heavy eyebrows, a prominent nose, and a black drooping mustache. When he smiled, there was little humor in it, but it rather came across as a cynical sneer. He was also a man with a quick temper that he displayed to anyone or anything that annoyed him.

Doc studied him for a minute, finally shrugged his shoulders, and walked back to his office.

That afternoon Marty Fitzpatrick was in the Red Rose Saloon, nursing a shot of whisky. He had just finished a temporary job at the holding pens for a trail herd that had come up from Texas. The corrals in Wichita were filled, so they had moved on up to Newton. He still wore his working denims and jacket, which concealed the .44 Smith and Wesson in the belt at his back.

As he swirled the reddish liquid in is glass, he was thinking how dull things were becoming in Newton. He should have moved on to Wichita several months ago, or maybe west to Dodge. He was hearing that that little town was wide open.

Contributing to his restlessness were the activities of last evening. The faro dealer at the Red Rose had spotted a free spender who had drifted into town and had passed the information on to Marty. Marty gave him a small commission on these tips. Marty kept his eye on the stranger all evening, and when he finally decided to call it a night, Marty followed him outside. The streets were dark and deserted except for two cowboys who came out of the McAllister Saloon and started walking north. They appeared a little unsteady on their feet and were singing in loud voices about a girl named Lou.

Marty moved up behind the stranger, and as they passed an alley, he pulled the large revolver from the back of his belt and brought it down hard on the stranger's head. The man slumped to the ground without a sound, and Marty pulled him into the narrow passage between the buildings. He was just about to search him for his valuables when someone came running down the street shooting his gun in the air and yelling. Marty recognized him by his voice: Sheriff Brooks. The sheriff must have seen Marty hit the man and was now charging toward him. Marty sprinted out of the backside of the alley, hoping that the sheriff hadn't been able to see who he was. It had been a close call, and Marty felt lucky to have gotten away.

Yup. Time he thought about moving on. Newton just wasn't the free-wheeling town it had been a year ago.

Marty's thoughts were interrupted when the front doors of the saloon were slammed open. Buck stood in the entrance, wearing two guns in holsters tied to his legs.

His face had a grim, hard look as his eyes adjusted to the dim light inside. He spotted Marty at the end of the bar and started toward him, his lips curled in an ugly snarl.

A wave of fear swept through Marty. *He knows*, he thought. *He knows I killed his ma and pa. That damned old man must have blabbered.*

Marty took a step or two back as Buck drew nearer. He was terrified. He knew he couldn't beat Buck in a shootout.

"You stinking bit of sheep dung," Buck said. "You killed my parents. Shot them down in cold blood. I should have put you out of your miserable hide long time ago. But I'm going to do it now. You're a dead man, Marty."

Marty was desperate. ""What do you mean?" he said in a voice trembling with panic.

"You know full well what I mean. You are the most despicable excuse for a man I've ever seen."

"No, no. You've got it all wrong. It was that old man Gramps what did the killing. If he said it was me, he was lying to save his own hide."

"Are you asking me whom I would believe between Gramps and you? That's the laugh of the day. And anyway, he wasn't trying to save his hide, as you put it. It was a deathbed confession."

"I haven't got a gun," Marty said in a pleading voice, a bead of sweat breaking out on his forehead. "You can't shoot an unarmed man."

Buck pulled the pistol out of the holster on his left side, pulled back the trigger, and laid it on the counter beside Marty. "You've got one now, Marty, and it's cocked and ready to fire. Anytime you're ready."

"It wouldn't be fair. I can't beat you, Buck. Please, let me go." Marty was hysterical. He fell to his knees and soiled his pants.

Buck glared at the man trembling before him. All he had been able to think about since leaving Gramps was getting even with the killer of his parents. He had spent five years trying to find who it was, and now he had him.

"Marty, you might as well stand up and go for the gun 'cause I'm going to kill you whether you do or not. Get on your feet, you sniveling coward!"

But as he said this, another image flashed in his mind, replacing that of his parents. It was of Katrina, begging him not to kill Marty. He tried to push this picture away as his hand moved toward the gun hanging at his side, but it kept coming back. The picture of Katrina imploring him to let the law handle this filled his mind. Then a voice from deep within seemed to say, "You know that killing this hombre will not make you feel better. Think of your wife. Her love is much more important than seeking personal revenge on this miserable excuse of a man."

Buck paused, and after a minute, his whole body seemed to sag as the anger drained out of him.

"For crying out loud," he muttered. "You are so miserable it isn't even worth wasting a bullet on you. We'll try it Katrina's way and let the law deal with you. We have witnesses to what Gramps said."

He picked up the revolver still lying on the counter, carefully released the trigger, and returned it to his holster. Giving Marty one last look of disgust, he turned and started for the door.

Marty's first reaction was one of tremendous relief. He had been spared. But this was quickly followed by a towering rage. Still on his knees, he reached back and pulled his .44 from the back of his belt. Holding it with two hands, he drew a bead on Buck's back.

Two shots rang out in quick succession. Buck swirled around at the twin blasts, whipping his gun out, and falling to a kneeling position.

Marty was leaning back against the bar, sitting with a surprised expression on his face, still holding the pistol. A crimson flow began to appear on his chest, and it looked like he was trying to say something. Then he slumped onto his side and was still.

Sheriff Brooks was at the other end of the bar, his pistol still smoking. "Wasn't going to interfere with a fair contest," he said, "but I can't tolerate a back shooter. Guess we won't have to worry now whether Gramps's testimony would have been admitted in a court or not."

Buck looked back at Marty. It was over, finally over after all these years. *I should feel elated*, he thought. *Or vindicated or even satisfied.* But he felt none of these things, only a desire to get back to Katrina and their farm.

Chapter 21

"Ted, would you take a look at this?" Martha King asked. She was standing behind the counter at the bakery, having just sold a loaf of bread to a construction worker, and was examining the bill he had offered in payment. "I've never seen one of these before."

Ted walked over, took the piece of paper she was holding, and held it up to the light. "It looks like money," he said, "but it's not issued by the government. Federal government anyway. Says it is redeemable for one dollar in US currency and is a promissory note by Harvey County."

He turned to the customer, who was a Mexican still dressed in dirty working clothes. "Where did you get this?" he asked.

"I work for the county," he replied, "and this is what they pay me with. They tell me it is as good as regular money."

Ted handed the bill back to Martha. "It's what they call a warrant, or scrip," he said. "Sometimes states or counties, or even companies, who have a lot of fixed assets but a cash flow problem will issue these. They are treated just like regular money, as long as everyone has confidence in the ability of the issuer to make good on them. Go ahead and accept it, but I sure haven't heard anything about the county doing this."

Just then Jenny came into the store holding three bills, one for a dollar and two for five dollars. She saw the scrip Martha was holding and said, "I see you've gotten these, too. Do you think they're any good?" she asked Ted.

"Probably, at least here in Harvey County. Doubt that anyone would accept them elsewhere though."

"When did all of this come about?" Jenny said. "I certainly haven't heard anything about the county printing up money on their own."

"Same here," Ted replied. "I wonder just how much they've issued and who authorized it. There's a county commissioner meeting tomorrow night. I think I'll plan to be there for that one."

"How's Linda?" Jenny asked. "Getting excited over the big wedding date?"

"Yeah, I guess," Ted said. "Although it's still a ways off."

"You two sure believe in long engagements. I would have thought with anyone that pretty that you'd be eager to get married."

"We've known each other since we were little kids, so it's not like we just now fell in love. Besides, I think she still hopes that if she delays long enough I will give in and move back east. Anyway, I'm glad I'm not back there right now for all of the hoopla of getting ready— invitations, flowers, wedding dress. I wish we could just elope and forget about all the rest."

Jenny chuckled. "That's a man for you. Don't you know that getting married is one of the biggest events in your life?"

"I'm learning. And how are things between you and Alan? Has he popped the question yet?"

Jenny turned a bright red. "Alan? He's just a friend, Ted. There's nothing between us."

"I think you might have a hard time convincing him of that."

When many of the saloons and gambling places pulled out of Newton for Wichita, they left behind quite a few abandoned buildings. One of these had been converted to temporary offices for the county. On this night, the commissioners were meeting in a conference room in that building with a crowd of angry citizens. Although the matter of the scrip issued by the county was not on the agenda, it became the focal point of questions from the audience, and the commissioners were forced to address the issue. Ted Baker was one of the more vocal participants.

"I can understand the necessity of the county issuing these warrants," Ted said to County Supervisor Wally Tomney. "It is a fairly common practice out here in the west, but this comes as a surprise to all of us merchants and business people. The acceptance of these warrants as legal tender depends on the confidence we have in the county to make good on them. Don't you think it would have been a good idea to have discussed this in open meetings before you acted?"

"I didn't see the necessity of that then nor do I now," Tomney replied. "The county commissioners, in consultation with the county treasurer and other elected officials, have full authority to manage the county's financial affairs as they deem necessary."

"But I understand from talking to some of them that they weren't aware that the county was actually preceding with the project. I was told that the plan had been discussed as a possibility, but they hadn't made a decision yet on how much or when to start."

"I would like to know, sir, just who has made such statements to you," Tomney replied angrily.

"It doesn't matter who told me this," Ted said. He wasn't about to disclose the source of the comment and get that person in trouble with the county's political machine. "We can just look at the minutes of the meeting of the commissioners when a vote was taken. They should be in the public domain and should answer all of our questions. Will you provide us with those minutes?"

Tomney was red-faced with anger, but he turned to the commissioners. "I don't know if we have any minutes or not. Are you gentlemen aware of any minutes when we made the decision to go ahead?"

Nobody spoke, and several nodded their heads in the negative.

"I guess that settles that," Tomney said.

"No minutes? You can't be serious. The county decides to issue scrip in what I would guess is in the tens of thousands of dollars, and there are no minutes? That sounds negligent almost to the point of being criminal."

"Now you look here, young man," Tomney shouted. "You don't understand how a county government has to work. We can't call meetings every day to run the public affairs. Oftentimes there is no meeting at all. I just contact the commissioners at their places of business, and we verbally agree on things. We don't need minutes and all that bureaucracy to run this government."

"Well, then can you tell us how much scrip has been issued? And how much is still on hand?"

"I don't keep track of things like that," Tomney retorted. "I suppose someone might know. We use whatever is needed to meet payrolls and county expenses."

"So you are telling me," Ted said in an even but forceful voice, "that this county has issued scrip in some unknown amount that may or may not have been authorized, and there are no records of any of this?"

"I am not going to stand up here and be harassed by your insinuations," Tomney said. "It is obvious you are only trying to make trouble for reasons of your own, and I'm not going to be a part of your charade." Tomney stormed from the meeting, and after a minute, the rest of the commissioners followed in the midst of boos and catcalls from the audience.

CHAPTER 22

The black carriage, pulled by a single roan horse, sported a red leather two-seater and four wheels in a matching shade. The fold-back top was up, shading the driver from the warm, summer sun.

Horse and buggy came up the roughly graded road to the Dorsky farm and pulled to a stop at the front door. The driver, a man in his late twenties, stepped down and tied the horse to the hitching post as Martin Dorsky came from the house.

"Bernhard," he exclaimed. "My old friend! Welcome to our home." Looking back to the house, he called out, "Anna! Come see who is here. Bernhard Warkentin."

The two men embraced warmly and went inside.

Bernhard Warkentin was a tall man with a full black mustache and beard. His dark hair was receding a bit from his forehead, but a cowlick came down with a slight curl over his right eye. His easy movements indicated an agile and supple body full of energy.

After the guest was comfortably seated in the living room parlor and provided with a cup of cold tea, Martin asked, "So tell me. Is not the land everything I have written to you about?"

"Indeed it is," Bernhard responded. "I have traveled all over the middle part of this new nation, from Minnesota to the Dakotas down to here. I think the soil and climate here are almost identical to that of our home in Ukraine. It will be good wheat country."

"And have you taken steps to buy any land yet?"

"Yes, at Halstead, fifteen miles to the west of Newton. The Little Arkansas River flows through the village, and it will be the perfect place to build my gristmill. It will be started by the end of the month."

"Excellent. Have you brought with you any of our Turkey Red hard winter wheat seeds to plant?"

"Only a few barrels. But it will be enough to confirm our belief that the wheat will do exceptionally well here."

"So you think our Kansas maybe has a good future?"

"Martin, I believe this state and this community has a wonderful prospect in store for it. And I intend to do everything I can to be a part of that growth. I am already planning to build a second mill in Newton. Furthermore, it is not too soon to be thinking about a bank. And who knows what may lie next? A hospital, maybe? Or even a college?"

Dorsky laughed. "Bernard," he said, "that is the thing I love about you. You do not have the small, ordinary dream. You have dreams bigger than the ocean. When most people look at a field and envision a crop growing on it, you see not only the crop but a city behind it with railroads and schools and tall buildings."

"Ah, but for these dreams to become reality there must be people. People who are honest and hard-working, and frugal and willing to take a chance. And we both know of just such ones."

"Our brothers in Russia who are planning to come to this country. You have been in contact with them?"

"Yes, but unfortunately they have made up their minds to settle to the north, in Nebraska."

"That is a shame. They are good people and good farmers. They would be a blessing to our community. You must keep after them to change their decision."

"I will try, but I think it is not possible."

———————————

It was getting on to the latter part of June in 1873 when Pete Richards rode into Newton. "Anybody seen Arthur McCluskie?" he asked every person he saw on the boardwalk or crossing the dirt street. "A big fellow, coal-black hair and gray-black beard?"

On the fifth try, he found someone who knew him.

"Saw him down at Tuttle's Saloon a short time ago. Reckon he's still there."

Pete entered the tavern a few minutes later, paused at the door while his eyes adjusted to the dim light, and spotted McCluskie in a poker game in a corner of the room. He sauntered over to the table and in between hands addressed Arthur.

"Art, I have news about a friend of yours, a fellow you've been hoping to catch up with for two years now. Name of Anderson. Hugh Anderson."

McCluskie, who was dealing the cards, stopped in midstride. "You gonna tell me you know where he is?"

"Tending bar at Harding's Trading Post in Medicine Lodge. Seen him myself."

McCluskie sat for a moment without moving, his eyes taking on a faraway look. Then he threw the cards on the table. "I'm out, boys. Got me some unfinished business to attend to, a promise I made to my dead brother."

A week later McCluskie and Richards were on the outskirts of Medicine Lodge, which was little more than a trading post for hunters and Indians. Six years earlier it had been the site of a large peace meeting with the Arapaho, Comanche, Prairie Apache, Kiowa, and Cheyenne tribes. The hillside had been covered with over five hundred Indian lodges, the tribes meeting with General Harney and a peace delegation from Washington. Two hundred troops from the US 7th Cavalry accompanied the group. Down this same dusty street, Tall Bull and the Cheyenne Dog Soldiers had put on a display of military-like precision on their horses that had impressed everyone there.

A peace treaty had been signed in which the Indians relinquished all claim to their lands in Kansas and Nebraska, but they did not fully realize what they were putting their mark to, and the conflict with the Cheyenne continued for four more years.

None of this was in McCluskie's thoughts as he stared down the empty road. There was nobody in sight, although seven horses were tied up in front of the trading post.

McCluskie pulled a fourteen-inch Bowie knife from its scabbard and ran his finger along the edge. "Richards," he said, "I want you to go into the store, and if Anderson is there, let him know I'm here. I'll give him the choice of weapons, guns or knives—or both. Personally I'd prefer knives. I'd get much more satisfaction in driving this here blade deep into his guts and twisting it once it was in, but since I'm the one calling him out, I'll let him make the choice. But be sure to tell him who I am and why I'm here."

McCluskie slid off his horse, tied him to a hitching post, and checked his gun while Richards strode to the saloon-trading post. Inside he found Anderson working at the bar. There were a half dozen people in the room, sitting at tables, smoking cigars, drinking whiskey, and playing cards. Richards walked over to the counter.

"Howdy, cowboy," Anderson said. "What will it be?"

"You're Anderson? Hugh Anderson?"

Hugh eyed him with suspicion. "I am. Why do you ask?"

"I got a message for you. From Arthur McCluskie, Mike McCluskie's brother. Name mean anything to you?"

"I reckon I might have heard the name before. What's the message?"

"Arthur's outside in the street waiting for you. Said for you to choose the weapon, guns or knives. He don't care which."

Anderson placed both hands on the counter and didn't say anything for a few minutes. He somehow knew this day would come. He had heard that Arthur was a big man, so he wasn't about to choose knives for the duel. Finally he said, "Tell your friend it will be guns. I don't even own a knife. I'll be out in a minute, soon as I close things down here."

Turning to the rest of the men in the room, he said, "Drink up, boys. The bar is closing. Going to be some excitement out in the street in a few minutes. A fellow thinks he's got a score to settle with me. I had to put his brother out of his miserable life a few years ago, and now I 'spect I'll have to do the same for this gent."

One of the customers, Red Bond, had overheard the message Richards had delivered to Anderson. He walked up to Hugh and pulled out his knife. In case you want it, it's a Hunter knife, made in Newark. Got a seven-inch blade."

"Thanks, but I think I'll stick to the gun."

Jake Harding, the owner of the trading post, came up to Anderson. "You don't have to do this, son. Head out the back door and hit leather. I'll stall the hombre as long as I can."

"No, Jake. It's something that has to be settled. I don't aim to spend the rest of my life looking over my shoulder, wondering when he might show up again. I figure I'm a better shot than he is anyway."

"Then I'll be your second. Better check your gun."

A few minutes later Anderson and McCluskie faced each other in the street.

"Anderson, you're a low-down, good-for-nothin' skunk, and I aim to put you out of your misery and revenge my brother's murder. You're not going to leave this street alive."

"You McCluskies all smell alike. I'd have recognized you anywhere by the odor. Let's get on with it."

Harding stepped in between the two glowering gunmen. "All right, boys. I want each of you to stand back to back. You will step out twenty paces, and when I say 'now,' you will turn and fire at will. If anyone breaks early, I'll shoot him myself. Any questions?"

A sizeable crowd had gathered on the sidelines, and bets were flying as to who would win. The two antagonists stood with their backs to each other, and then each stepped out twenty paces as directed. After they were in position and ready, Harding called out, "*Now!*"

Both men turned and began firing. Neither was hit after the first volley, but McCluskie's second shot hit Anderson in the left arm. He fell to the ground on his knees but kept shooting and one of his bullets ripped through McCluskie's mouth. It was not a fatal wound however, and after spitting out blood and broken teeth, McCluskie gave a roar and charged toward Anderson, who was still on his knees. Anderson continued firing, and two of his shots hit home—one in McCluskie's leg and another in his stomach. That should have ended the fight, but somehow McCluskie, now lying prone on the ground, got a shot off that hit Anderson in the midsection, knocking him backward on the dusty street. Both men had used up all of their bullets in the exchange.

The crowd watched in amazement as McCluskie, bleeding profusely, pulled his knife from his belt and began crawling toward Anderson.

"Stop the fight. That's enough," someone in the crowd hollered, but Harding kept the onlookers back.

"It's a fight to the finish, boys, and we're not going to intervene."

Red Bond pulled his knife from his belt and threw it at the feet of Anderson. "Looks like you might be needing this after all," he said.

McCluskie was fading fast, but still he inched on, holding his knife in front of him. Anderson pushed himself into a sitting position and watched through cloudy, bloodshot eyes as McCluskie came on. Several times McCluskie slumped flat on the ground, his face in the dust, but then he raised his head, and started pushing forward. The sweat rolled off Anderson's face as he clutched his side with his left hand and steadied himself with his right on the ground. As McCluskie drew near, Anderson pulled Bond's knife from the ground and clutched it in his right hand.

When they were but a few feet apart, McCluskie pushed himself back onto his knees. Both men glared at each other with hate-filled eyes, but neither spoke. Suddenly McCluskie lunged and drove his knife into Anderson's side, while at the same time Anderson brought his knife across McCluskie's throat. Both men fell back, McCluskie with his legs under him. He jerked several times in convulsions and then was still. Anderson was flat on his back and then rolled over on his side in a fetal position and did not move.

After a few minutes, Harding stepped out from the crowd and walked over to the combatants. He knelt down and felt for the pulse in McCluskie's wrist and then did the same for Anderson. He raised his head and announced to the crowd, "They're both dead. Done each other in."

The crowd that had been boisterous a few minutes earlier and excited about seeing a shootout was now quiet and sickened by the spectacle that had played out before them. All bets were called off, and they silently dispersed.

Chapter 23

The discontent with the county government continued for most of 1873. Protest meetings were held almost weekly, many of them headed by Ted Baker.

Late one evening in December, Tomney was sitting in his office nursing a tall glass of Kentucky whiskey. He was furious over a confrontation earlier in the day with Baker.

A soft knock came at the door, and it opened without waiting for a reply. A tall man in wrangling clothes came into the office. He had a round face covered by a scrubby beard that hadn't been shaved for a week. His eyes were small and beady.

"Hello, Conan," Tomney said. "Come on in."

"Heard it around that you might have a job for me," Conan replied.

"I do. I trust I can rely on your complete secrecy and loyalty?"

"I haven't disappointed you so far have I? What's on your mind?"

"There's a business in town, Ted's Bakery, that needs some modifications to its structure. I would deem it advantageous if this shop was somehow rendered unable to continue its operation."

"That's a lot of words just to say you want me to kill the owner."

"No, no. I don't want any harm to come to anyone. I must be very clear on that point. I just want his bakery destroyed—the ovens and furniture. I need for Mr. Baker to start worrying more about his own business and less about mine. My hope is that this might persuade Baker to leave our little city."

"I reckon I could take care of that. If the price is right, that is."

"There's two hundred dollars in it for anyone that wants the job. Payable when the assignment is completed."

"You got your man, Tomney. Have that money ready by the end of the week."

———

Two days later Ted was up at four thirty in the morning and headed for the shop to start up the ovens. As he neared the building, he heard hammering and crashing sounds from inside. He opened the door and rushed into the shop. There was a dim light in the back room, with more sounds of things being smashed. Ted ran to the back room and looked in.

A kerosene lamp disclosed a large man with a heavy sledgehammer, like the ones used by railroad crews for driving spikes, swinging away at the tables and shelving. The ovens had already been battered to little more than clay and metal scraps.

Ted raced to the intruder, charging into him before the man could swing around with the mallet. Both bodies slammed against the wall, and the man dropped the hammer with a grunt of pain. While the man was temporarily stunned, Ted threw a right fist into his face, hitting him square on the nose, which immediately spurted blood. It was a blow that would have floored most men, but the intruder merely shook his head and with a roar started battering Ted with both fists.

The fight was hard and vicious, but it was soon apparent that Ted was no match for his larger opponent. Then Conan connected with an uppercut squarely on Ted's chin, and Ted smashed back against the table with the kerosene lamp. The lamp went flying across the room, spilling its contents on the floor. The room caught fire.

Ted tried to lift himself up, but the effort was too much. Everything turned blurry and then dark as he collapsed. He lay unmoving only a few feet from the flames now growing in size and intensity. In only a few minutes, the south wall was completely on fire, and the inferno was spreading to the roof.

Conan stared at the room for a moment, trying to stop the flow of blood from his nose and rubbing his bruised jaw. *Tomney didn't want anyone hurt*, he thought. *But if this coyote burns up in an accident, I don't think he'll be too unhappy.* Conan turned and rushed out the front door.

Pedro lay in bed, reluctant to rise and start his busy day at the bakery. He rolled on his side and gazed at the peaceful profile of his wife, Anita. They had been married for a month now, and Pedro had never been happier. Finally he edged to the side of the bed and got up and dressed, careful not to awaken her. He didn't bother with coffee or breakfast. He would get these at work.

As soon as he stepped outside, he could smell the smoke that hung heavy in the air. Then he saw the glow in the sky, which was still dark, and realized a fire must be burning very close to their shop. He set off at a fast walk, which quickly changed to a run as he drew nearer and realized his fears were well founded.

Three men were on the street outside of Ted's Bakery, watching as flames engulfed the building.

"Wake everyone up!" yelled one of the trio. "Bob, you go to the homes to the south. I'll go west. John, you hit the houses to the east. We've got to get enough people to form a fire brigade, getting water from our well."

Pedro grabbed the one called Bob and asked, "Have you seen Senor Ted, the man that owns this shop?"

"Haven't seen anyone but us three," he said, and he rushed off into the darkness.

Pedro gazed at the burning buildings for a moment. He knew Ted was always in the shop at this time of the morning. *Could he be in that inferno now?* The roof was blazing brightly, and the south wall looked like it was about to collapse in burning embers.

Suddenly Pedro made up his mind and dashed into the shop, ducking his head under blazing timbers and sidestepping around leaping flames on the walls. The room was filled with thick smoke, making Pedro's eyes burn and his throat constrict. Trying to shield his head with his arms, he searched for any sight of Ted and then saw him lying prone on the floor, the raging fire only a few feet away. He rushed over, knelt down, and lifted Ted's head.

"Senor, you must get up. There is no time." He shook Ted violently. Slowly Ted forced his eyes open and tried to focus on his assistant.

"Pedro," he muttered. "Have I been shot again? Haven't we been through this before?"

"I don't know about a bullet, my friend, but your face looks like it has been run over by many buffalo. You must get up. Now!"

Ted looked around and for the first time realized they were in an inferno, with fire all around and burning timbers falling from the roof. He struggled to his feet, and Pedro, supporting him, led the way through the flames to the front door. Both men were gagging from the smoke when they emerged into the open. They welcomed the cool fresh air with deep breaths while trying to rid their lungs of the acid fumes.

The fire had spread to other offices to the north and south, and the entire block of businesses were being consumed by the dancing, angry flames. A fire brigade was hauling water from the town well, but the efforts were not doing much good. The inferno roared on for over an hour before finally dying out at each end of the block. Eleven businesses were destroyed.

Ted stood in front of the shambles that had once been his bakery as bright rays of the morning sun began to come up from the east, illuminating the smoking, charred ruins. There was nothing left.

"Oh, Ted. I am so very sorry." Jenny had come from nowhere and was standing by his side. "You've lost everything," she said with a slight quiver in her voice. Ted looked at her, and even though her eyes were glazed over with tears, he thought how beautiful she was.

"Marry me," he said without any preamble.

"Wh-what?" Jenny looked closely at him, sure that she had not heard correctly. He gazed down at her, his face covered with bruises and soot and hair flopping over his forehead.

"Jenny, I love you. Will you marry me?"

"Ted, I think you must be in shock. You'd better lie down. You may have a concussion."

"Not till you answer me. Will you marry me?"

Jenny stared at him in disbelief, trying to determine if he was serious.

"Ted, I'm warning you. You say that one more time and I'm liable to accept, and then where—"

"Jenny, I have loved you from the moment I first laid eyes on you. You are all I can think about. When things are wonderful, you are the one I want by my side. And when things are rough, like now, you are all I care about. All of this"—he pointed at the pile of ashes that had once been his shop—"are just things. I can start a new batch of sourdough. All of this can be replaced. You are the important thing in my life."

"Oh, Ted. Yes, yes, yes, I will marry you."

He pulled her to him, and their lips met in a long, passionate kiss. Minutes later Jenny pulled back. "But what about Linda?" she asked. "You are supposed to be going back to marry her at the end of the month. What will you tell her?"

"The truth. You are the one I love. I expect she will be as relieved as me. I don't think either one of us is really in love with the other. We grew up in this small town, and everyone took it for granted that we would get married. I guess we kinda went along with it all, even though we weren't that enamored with each other. It won't take her long to get over it."

"I love you so much, Ted. Ever since that first day you came looking for the new postmaster. But I thought you were already taken and didn't dare let myself think about it."

Ted let his gaze sweep over the simmering ruins once more.

"This is the happiest day in my life," he said with a big grin.

CHAPTER 24

The fire in 1873 set business back in Newton, but by spring of the next year, rebuilding was well underway. Ted's Bakery reopened in a store two blocks further north with a state-of-the-art stopped-end steam oven. Pedro was made part owner of the shop. Ted and Jenny were married with Buck McNurty as best man and Katrina the maid of honor. Voters were about to throw Tomney and the old political machine out of office. Things were looking decidedly rosy for the town, and then disaster struck.

It was a hot, humid day in August 1874. Ted was at his shop but seemed distracted, his mind somewhere else.

"I think there is a thing that you worry about," Pedro said. "You have only listened to half my talk. Are things not well with you?"

"Oh, things are fine. Fine," Ted replied. Then after a pause said, "Actually, you are right, Pedro. It's Jenny. She has not been well for the last week. I am worried about her."

"Has she seen the doctor?" Pedro asked.

"Seeing him as we speak." Ted pulled his watch out of his pocket and looked at it. "In fact, she ought to be through by now. I think I'll run home and see what she found out. I'll be right back."

Ted headed out in the bright sun and started off at a brisk pace. He was thinking about Jenny, praying that she was all right. He absentmindedly brushed a large grasshopper off his arm as he hurried along. Jenny had been ill for almost a week and had thrown up on several occasions.

As he neared his home, another grasshopper ran into his forehead. As he brushed it away, he noticed for the first time that there seemed to be an abnormally large number of the pests on the bushes and on the sidewalk.

When he reached his home, he rushed inside and found Jenny sitting in the living room, her eyes red from crying. He stopped in his tracks, blood draining from his face.

"Jenny, what is it? What did the doctor say? Does he know what is wrong?"

Jenny looked at him and mustered a tiny smile. "Yes. It is just what I expected. But I needed him to say it."

Ted's heart seemed to stop, and he had difficulty speaking. "What is it? What did he say?"

Jenny's smile got bigger. "We're going to have a baby," she said. "I'm pregnant."

Ted stood for a full minute, trying to digest what she had just said. Then he let out a loud yell. "We're going to have a baby? That's all that is wrong?"

"Isn't that enough? What did you expect?"

"But you have been crying. Your eyes are red."

"Crying from happiness. Oh, Ted, I am so excited."

Ted grabbed her and held her tight. "What wonderful news," he finally said. "I was so worried. I was afraid... I guess I don't know what I thought. But we're gong to have a baby! I'm going to be a father!" Ted let out another loud yell and spun Jenny around in a half circle and then stopped suddenly.

"But shouldn't you be resting? Should you be on your feet?" He helped her to the divan and almost pushed her down. "What can I do?"

Jenny laughed. "Ted, it's going to be eight months. Better not start treating me like an invalid already."

Twenty minutes later Ted took off for the shop, eager to tell everyone the good news.

As he stepped outside, he noticed the grasshoppers on the dusty street and in the grass. They seemed to be everywhere. When he was still a block from the shop, the sky turned dark. He looked up and saw a huge cloud of the locusts in the sky, completely blocking the sun. They began to drop all around him, and as he walked, they crunched under his feet. By time he got to the bake shop, he was covered with the insects. Trying to brush them off, he went inside.

Martin Dorsky and his wife were in the fields admiring their first crop of corn.

"It isn't what you might call the great crop," Martin was saying, "but it will get us through this winter."

"You have done well, my husband. We cannot expect too much in our very first year. But look at those bugs on that stalk over there. They are all over the ears of corn."

Martin laughed. "Do not worry, my darling. They are but a few grasshoppers, and as one of God's creatures are entitled to a little sustenance. But they will not eat so very much."

He walked over to the corn and brushed the winged feasters away, then did a double take on the ears of corn that had been stripped bare.

"I think maybe these particular creatures have been a little greedy, though," he muttered.

As Martin looked more closely at his crop he became aware for the first time that the grasshoppers seemed to be everywhere across the field. *This is not too good*, he thought.

As they turned to make their way back to the house Martin noticed a dark cloud in the sky. "Look, Anna. Maybe we will get that rain we need so badly. It has been a dry summer."

Mrs. Dorsky studied the fast approaching mass in the sky. "Martin," she said, "I do not think it is a cloud. It is something else."

"Merciful God," Martin said a few minutes later. "Those are grasshoppers. Millions and millions of grasshoppers."

Buck and Katrina were in their house sipping a cold cup of coffee when the grasshoppers arrived. In the hot dog days of August, they had learned to enjoy their beverages cold—or at least as cold as it gets in 100 degree temperatures. They were talking about the success of their harvest when they became aware of a thumping on the roof, sounding like a heavy rainstorm, and a sudden darkening of the sunlight outside.

Buck walked to the door and peered out. "My God," he said. "Look at this! Grasshoppers! Everywhere!" He looked toward the barn and the piles of corn he had just harvested. They were covered with hundreds of the insects. They're eating all the corn." He grabbed a broom and rushed outside, Katrina following. The locusts were an inch thick on the ground and crunched under his feet as he ran. He reached the corn and tried to beat them off with the broom, but it had little effect. For every bug he knocked off, three more took its place.

In the barn, the horses were crying out in long drawn-out neighing.

"I will see to the horses," Katrina said, and she rushed into the building. It was a small enclosure, with two stalls on the right and bales of straw and equipment on the left. Grasshoppers were over everything eatable, their little jaws working rapidly away.

They had two horses, one a black and white stallion and the other a reddish brown mare. Both animals were covered with the insects and were frantic trying to shake them off. Katrina opened the door to the first stall and rushed in to try and calm the mare. The horse looked at her with bulging, fear-ridden eyes as she tried to brush the grasshoppers off its back.

"Easy, girl, easy," she said. A saddle blanket was draped over the side railing, and she grabbed it and threw it over the animal's back. It was immediately covered with the ravenous locusts.

The stallion in the next stall was rubbing hard against the side of the barn in an attempt to dislodge the insects. It looked at Katrina with swollen eyes, as if begging her to do something. Katrina backed out of the first stall, closed the gate, grabbed another blanket, and entered the second stall.

As she approached the animal, holding the blanket up to put on his back, the horse reared up on its hind legs, its forepaws flaying wildly in the air. One of them hit Katrina on the shoulder and knocked her down. The hoofs came down hard and then were raised in the air once again as the frantic horse tried to free itself from the locusts. Over and over the pony rose on its hind legs as it pawed at the door to the stall. There was such a loud buzzing from the insects that Buck didn't hear Katrina's calls.

The grasshopper plague was about the worst thing that could have happened to the fledging county. Crops were consumed right out of the ground. There were reports of clothing eaten off the backs of people caught in the onslaught and wool devoured off the backs of live sheep. The locusts were so thick that locomotives couldn't get enough traction to move because the rails were so slippery. There wasn't a green thing left anywhere. The trees and bushes were stripped and looked like the dead of winter.

There was no grain left anywhere, either to plant for the next year or to feed livestock.

Business was practically suspended. Many of the farmers were compelled to leave their farms to seek work elsewhere. Others left the country entirely and returned to the east, heart-sick over their losses. The stores in the city were hit hard because people no longer had money to spend.

It was a disaster of the worst magnitude.

———————

Ten days after Katrina's funeral, Buck appeared at Ted's Bakery. Ted had only to take one look to know he was leaving. He no longer wore farming clothes, but had donned his western gear, including the guns strapped to his side.

"Reckon I'll be heading back to Texas," Buck said. "Just wanted to drop in and say goodbye. You've been a real friend."

"Buck, you don't need to leave. Things will get better. If you need a loan to buy grain, I might be able to help out some."

"It isn't that, Ted. With Katy gone, there just doesn't seem to be any point to anything anymore. There's certainly no reason for me to sit out on that farm and try to make something out of it. Who would I do that for? For me? What joy is there in that?"

Ted thought about Jenny and how devastated he would be if anything were to happen to her.

"When you've found someone you love more than life," Buck continued, "and you've planned together and dreamed together, and suddenly that part of your life is ripped away, there just isn't much left to care about."

"Katrina was a wonderful woman," Ted said. "And you have been a good husband to her. You certainly earned her love."

"No. I didn't earn or even deserve her love. That was a gift she gave me, and it has made all the difference."

Ted tried to think of something to say, but the words wouldn't come. Finally he said, rather lamely, "What will you do down in Texas?"

"Guess I'll cross that bridge when I get to it. Punch cattle, I guess. Doesn't much matter. I've deeded the farm to Martin Dorsky. He's agreed to sell it for me. Not that anybody's got enough resources left to be buying land."

Looking out the door, Ted saw that Buck was riding Katrina's mare instead of the black and white stallion he usually rode. "What did you do with your other horse?" he asked, wondering at the same time if he really wanted to know.

"Got rid of him," Buck answered. "I couldn't bear to have him around after he…" Buck didn't finish the sentence. Seeing the questioning expression on Ted's face, he added, "No, I didn't shoot him. Although I sure thought about it. I gave him to a neighbor. Don't know how he's going to feed him, though. No grain left anywhere in the county."

While they talked, a farmer named Jake Patterson came into the store. He had a wagon outside loaded with his personal possessions and his wife and two children.

"Need to buy a couple loaves of bread," he said. "Got just enough money for that. Guess that's all we'll have to live on till we get back to my wife's family in St. Louis."

Ted wrapped up the bread and gave to the man. "The bread's on the house," Ted said. "Sorry to see you go. Things will get better if you could just stick it out."

"Have you taken a look around?" the man asked. "There's not a leaf left on any of the trees or bushes. The grass has been consumed by the devil locusts. They've eaten the wool off the backs of the sheep. Wooden handles on our tools, even clothing, have been consumed. The Lord has cursed this land, just like He did to Egypt."

"What do you mean?" Ted asked.

"It's in the Good Book," Jake replied. "The good Lord brought the locusts to Egypt as a curse to old Pharaoh." He lifted his eyes upwards and he began to recite in a deep baritone voice, "'The locusts came up over the land of Egypt. There had never been so many locusts. They covered the surface of the whole land so that the land was darkened and they ate every plant of the land and all the fruit of the trees and there was nothing green left.'

"It's clear to me that the Lord does not intend for us to settle in this wilderness," Jake continued, "and sent the locusts as a sign. It is cursed, and you would do well to leave."

Jake took the loaves of bread and left.

"About the way I feel," Buck said.

The door opened again, and Alan Basher came in, a wide grin on his face. "Good news!" he exclaimed. "The word of our disaster has spread to the east, and people are already sending relief supplies—beans, pork, and rice. And the railroad has agreed to transport all such supplies, and grain for feeding livestock and for planting, free of charge. I have been informed that already there are four railcars full of barley and corn on their way. And the governor and the legislature are meeting in a special session today to see what they can do."

"There you go, Buck," Ted said. "Help is on its way. Better stick around."

Buck smiled, probably his first smile since Katrina had died, but it was a rueful smile without any happiness behind it.

"That's good news all right. But it's not for me. I've no interest in farming anymore. Nor in much else, as far as that goes." Buck shook Ted's hand and left.

While Alan and Ted were discussing the news of help on its way, Martin Dorsky came in. He took a quick look around the shop and said, "I was hoping Buck might be here. I have the good news for him."

"We just heard," Ted said. "Carloads of grain and supplies being shipped from back east."

"Supplies? No, no. I speak of my fellow countrymen who are on their way to settle here. My good friend Bernhard Warkentin has been in touch with them and has convinced them to come to Kansas. They were going to settle in Nebraska, but he succeeded in changing their minds. There are three hundred families in Kansas City now who are coming here to Newton to buy land. They are prosperous farmers and have much money. They bring with them barrels and barrels of the Turkey Red winter wheat to plant. And Bernhard is opening a bank to help the farmers who are in such distress. Mr. Warkentin is going to save this community. I wanted to find Buck and try to change his mind about leaving for this Texas. His loss can be repaired."

"I don't think Buck is leaving because he lost his crop," Ted said. "He is leaving because he lost Katrina. Nothing can replace that."

Martin's enthusiasm faded. "Is true," he said sadly.

Chapter 25

Tomney sat at his desk, an unlit cigar hanging out of the side of his mouth. Sitting by his side was Charlie Zimmerman, the county treasurer. For the moment, neither man was speaking, each absorbed in his own thoughts.

Finally Charlie broke the silence. "We could hire some of the drifters down at Tuttle's bar to break up the crowd. Might even get them to do some harm to Baker and the other organizers." A rally was taking place at the corner of 6th and Main protesting the actions of the current county administration, with speeches by the candidates vowing to overthrow them in next week's election. Amos Prouty, a prominent citizen, was running against Tomney for the office of County Commissioner.

"You think I haven't considered that?" Tomney said angrily. "If I thought it would do any good, I would have put Mr. Baker away long ago. I figured when his bakery burned down he might pack up and leave our fair city. Didn't work out that way, though."

Charlie gave Tomney a furtive look. He had suspected that Tomney might have had something to do with the fire that destroyed not only Baker's place but an entire block of the city, but Tomney had never given any indication he was involved.

"Baker's their hero," Tomney continued. "Their knight in shining armor. If anything happened to him now, he would become a martyr. It's a lot safer for everyone to have a live hero than a dead martyr."

The two men sat in moody silence for several more minutes before Tomney spoke again. "No, Charlie, I think our time here is at an end. Election is next week, and we'll be shuttled right out of office. Time we moved on. Dodge City maybe, or some other little town on west."

"You don't think we can make a comeback here in Newton?"

"No, Charlie. We're done here. Newton has turned a corner. The wild wheeling and dealing days are over. It's becoming domesticated. People like Judge Muse and Ted Baker are taking over. I reckon we'd best be on our way."

AUTHOR'S NOTES

This book is a fictitious account of the early years of Newton, Kansas, but it is set in the backdrop of actual events in the town's history.

Judge R.W.P. Muse and D. L. Lakin determined the location of the town in 1870 in preparation for the AT&SF Railroad meeting with the famed Chisholm Trail. Judge Muse became a leading figure in the county and recorded much of what is contained in this book in his *History of Harvey County, Kansas 1871-1881*. This document has recently been republished by the Harvey County Historical Museum and Archives.

For a year and a half, Newton was the end of the trail for both the railroad and the cattle drives from Texas, and as a cow town it was boisterous, gaudy, and wild. Saloons, dance halls, and gambling establishments made up the greater part of the town. Other cities really did refer to the fledging community as "the wickedest town in the West."

The so-called Hyde Park Massacre as described is pretty much the way it happened, and the subsequent fight between Hugh Anderson and Arthur McCluskie is purportedly factual. Judge Muse believed that there were twelve men killed during those turbulent years, although some have estimated it was a much higher number. There is no count of the many shootings that did not result in death.

The exploits of Newton's first three sheriffs, Tom Carson, Carlos King, and William Brooks, are detailed in *Great Gunfighters of the Kansas Cowtowns 1867-1886* by Nyle Miller and Joseph Snell.

Tom Carson went back to Abilene after he left Newton and signed on as a deputy once more, but it wasn't long before he was in trouble again. He got into an argument with another deputy, Brocky Jack Norton, pulled his gun, and fired a warning shot, which accidentally hit a bartender in the hip. He was discharged from the police force that same month. He and Brocky Jack got into it again in January, and Carson shot him again. Carson was arrested and charged with attempted murder, but he and three other prisoners broke out of jail and lit out for Dodge City.

Marshall "Bully" Brooks was Newton's third sheriff, following the death of Carlos King. In an incident in 1872 he was shot three times by a couple of drunken cowboys. Undaunted, Brooks jumped on his horse and chased the pair for ten miles before finally deciding to return to Newton to have his wounds treated. He went to Ellsworth for a while after leaving Newton, where he did a little police work. Then he was hired as the Marshal in Dodge. He made quite a name for himself there, reportedly killing fifteen men and cleaning up the city.

He killed four men who were after him for shooting their brother—with one shot each, according to the story.

But like many a lawman, Brooks began to think he was the law instead of the man enforcing the law, and he started killing men under suspicious circumstances. After he shot a man over an argument about a lady that they were both interested in, the town decided they had enough of his kind of justice and let him go. It wasn't long after that before he tied in with a gang of horse and mule thieves, got arrested, and was strung up by a lynch mob.

In June of 1871, "a severe wind and rain storm swept over Harvey County and assuming the violence of a hurricane destroyed much property," according to Wm. G. Cutler's History of the State of Kansas. The same source describes "a terrific storm of hail, sleet and snow... destroying hundreds of cattle and occasioning much suffering" in October of the same year.

The break off of Harvey County from Sedgwick County occurred in 1872, prompted in part by the Republican Party cutting down the number of representatives Newton could have at their convention. Newton's early political system was fraught with corruption. Judge Muse writes:

> All this while the affairs of the county had been carelessly and badly (if not criminally) conducted. It was openly charged that a "Tweed Ring" had been formed, with headquarters in some of the county offices. It was also charged and generally believed that large amounts of money had been wrongfully issued in the form

of warrants, and paid without sanction of law…
but as the books had been loosely kept, and
in many cases no record whatsoever made of
important transactions…the matter was finally
dropped.

The fire in 1873 destroyed nearly all the east side of
block 38, the best business portion of the city. The cause
of the fire, however, is unknown.

The grasshopper scourge in 1874 came in "clouds so
thick and so ravenous as to eat up and destroy in two
or three weeks every stalk of corn and every vestige of
vegetation that was green enough for them to eat,"
according to Judge Muse. "This was the gloomiest period
in the history of the county."

The characters of Buck McNurty, Ted Baker, Jenny
Johnson, Katrina Dorsky, "Gramps" Thompson, Marty
Fitzpatrick, and Wally Tomney are all figments of the
author's imagination, but hopefully are representative of
the time and place.

The Mennonite immigrants and the Turkey Red
winter wheat they brought with them played a major role
in the development of the county. In 1870, Kansas had
raised less than 2.5 million bushels of spring wheat. In
1880, this had increased to 17.3 million bushels, and in
the peak year of 1997 almost 500 million bushels. We
have truly become the breadbasket of the world.

Bernhard Warkentin played an important role in this
growth. His letters to his home in the Ukraine made him
a leader of the Mennonites coming from Russia. He was

associated with the immigration department of the Santa Fe Railroad. At one time, one thousand Mennonites landed in New York, determined to go to Nebraska, but through Mr. Warkentin's efforts, they located in Kansas. He opened a second mill in Newton in addition to the one in Halstead, helped organize the Halstead State Bank in Halstead, the Kansas State Bank in Newton, and was instrumental in founding the Bethel Hospital in Newton, and Bethel College in North Newton.

Ironically, he died by a gunshot wound while traveling in the Holy Land. A young Turk, traveling in an adjoining compartment, accidentally discharged a pistol. The bullet penetrated the dividing wall of the compartment and struck Mr. Warkentin in the back. His home in Newton, the Warkentin House, is listed in the State and National list of Historic Places. He and his wife are interred in the family mausoleum in Newton, which he built just before his trip to the Holy Land.

The last buffalo to be killed in the county was in 1875.

Today the main street of Newton is also on the National and State Registers of Historic Districts. The city has come a long way from its rowdy and violent beginnings and, true to the vision of Judge Muse, offers, in the words of the Chamber of Commerce, "an ideal family environment: affordable, quiet neighborhoods, outstanding schools, and abundant community activities."

And its high school remembers its heritage, known proudly as the Newton Railroaders. If anyone is interested in learning more about Newton as a railroad town, I would recommend a book, *Newton, Kansas #1 Rail Hub 1871-1971* by Lucius Hurley.

Judge Muse wrote in his history of the county, "It is an old saying that a bad beginning ensures a good ending, and if this be true, then will the infamous character of our beginning foreshadow an after career of unexampled greatness and prosperity."